INDIRA AND OTHER STORIES

BANKIM CHANDRA CHATTERJEE

GYAN

Published by

Gyan Publishing House
5, Ansari Road
Daryaganj, New Delhi-110002
Phone: 011-47034999, 9811692060
E-mail: books@gyanbooks.com

Distribution Network
gyanbooks.com
India, USA, Canada, UK, Australia

ISBN: 978-93-7414-097-0 (PB)

First Published, 1918

2nd Impression 2026

Printed at: Gyan Press, Delhi.

INDIRA AND OTHER STORIES
Author: BANKIM CHANDRA CHATTERJEE

INDIRA AND OTHER STORIES

Indira and Other Stories

Bankim Chandra Chatterjee

INDIRA AND OTHER STORIES

BY
BANKIM CHANDRA CHATTERJEE
TRANSLATED BY
J. D. ANDERSON, I.C.S. (Retired)

with two coloured illustrations
BY
NANDALAL BOSE

CALCUTTA
MODERN REVIEW OFFICE
1918

CONTENTS.

ILLUSTRATIONS.

INDIRA

I.

At last I was being conveyed to my husband's home. My nineteenth birthday was past, and yet, contrary to Hindu customs, I had never left the home of my childhood. Why? The explanation is simple. My father was wealthy, my father-in-law poor. A few days after the wedding—I was only a child at the time—my father-in-law, in accordance with custom, sent people to fetch me away, but my father refused to part with me. "Let my son-in-law", he said, "first learn how to earn his own living. How can he maintain a wife under existing circumstances?" When this message was conveyed to my husband, he was much hurt and offended, (he was then only twenty years old), and he made a vow that he would set to work to earn a livelihood for us both. He set off for Western India. In those days there was no railway, and travel was difficult and dangerous. Nevertheless he made his way to the Punjab on foot, without means and without influence to help him. A young man who has the resolution to face perils and hardships is bound to overcome all obstacles. In a short time, he began to earn money, to make remittances. But for seven or eight years he neither returned home nor made any enquiries about me. Shortly before the period at which my tale begins, he had come home for the first time. The rumour ran that he had gained much wealth by taking contracts under the Commissariat. (Is that the right spelling, I wonder?) My father-in-law wrote to my father to say that Upendra (old-fashioned people must forgive me for thus boldly using my husband's name; I suppose ladies of the present day would not blush to say "my Upendra") had returned "by your worship's blessing", and was now in a position to maintain his wife. He had sent a palanquin and bearers. Would my father kindly send me to my new home? Or, if such were his orders, arrangements would be made for seeking a bride for Upendra elsewhere.

My father smiled to see that these were indeed newly enriched folk, with the manners of their kind. The palanquin was richly lined, over it was a silver canopy, the poles ended in grinning shark's heads in silver. The servant girl who had accompanied it was dressed in silk apparel, and had a fine gold bead on her necklet. Four stalwart black-bearded up-country retainers acted as escort.

My father, Hara Mohan Datta, was a gentleman by descent. He laughed and said, "My dearest Indira, I can keep you no longer. You must go now, but you must come back soon to see your old father. Mind you do not let all this magnificence make you conceited. In our homely Bengali phrase, do not smile at a finger posing as a banana tree!"[2]

So it was that I was at last on my way to my future home. My father-in-law's house at Manoharpur and my father's house at Mahespur were some twenty miles apart. So I rose early and took a hasty meal, knowing that however early we started it would be nightfall before we reached our journey's end. Halfway, there was a great lake of water known as the Black Tank, nearly a mile long, lying in the midst of lofty banks looking like hills, through which our road lay. The lake was surrounded by dense groves of ancient banyan trees. Its waters were as the dark thunderclouds in colour, very beautiful to look upon. The place was almost uninhabited. There was a single shop at the spot where travellers drew water when they halted by the lake. Not far distant was a little village, also called Kaladighi, after the Black Tank.

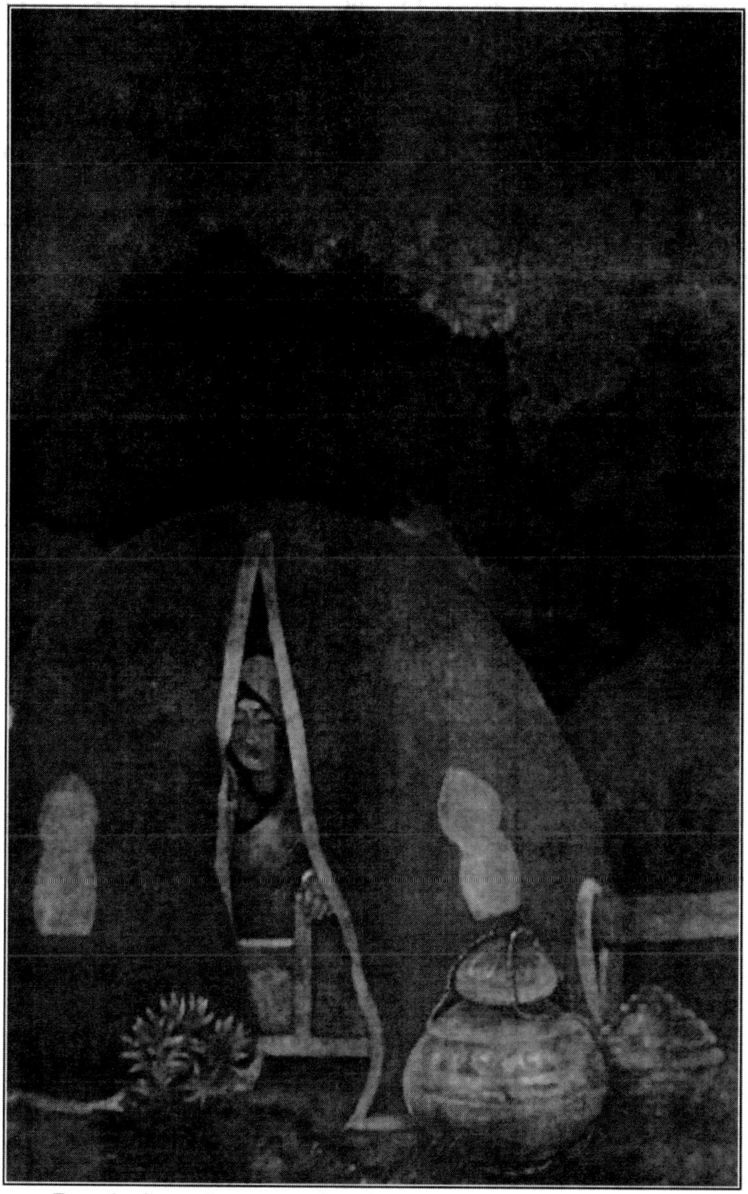

People feared to pass by this lake. The region had a bad repute for robbers, and travellers made up strong parties if they had to go this way. In fact the lake was commonly known as "Dakate Kaladighi", the Black Lake of the Dacoits. The solitary shopkeeper was suspected of being in league with thieves. As for me, I entertained no fears. There were many attendants with me—sixteen bearers, four armed retainers, and others as well. When we reached this place, it was already past mid-day. The bearers declared that they could not proceed further without stopping to eat and drink. My armed guards objected that the place had a bad name, but the bearers argued that with so numerous a party, there was no fear. All were fasting and weary, and finally a halt was resolved upon.

My palanquin was deposited close to the water's edge under the shade of the banyan trees. Presently I gathered from the sound of their voices that my attendants had gone to some distance. I summoned up courage to draw the sliding doors and look out on the lake. I saw that the bearers were taking their meal under a tree at a distance of about a hundred yards. Before me the lake spread its blue waters. Around it were the lofty yet rounded masses of the banks looking like hills; between them and the shore grew many mighty forest trees; on the slopes cattle were feeding; in the water the water-birds were joyously playing; a gentle breeze caused tiny waves to break in drops that glittered in the sunshine, and the lotuses rocked on the crest of the waves. I noticed that my armed guardians were in the water bathing. As they splashed they threw up drops that shone like diamonds in the brilliant rays of the afternoon sun. Then I observed that, with the exception of the bearers, all my attendants were in the water. Near me were only two helpless women, one my own maid, the other the woman my father-in-law had sent. I began to feel a little perturbed. There was no one near but my women. The place had an ill fame. I was fairly frightened. But what was I to do? A zenana lady, it was not for me to call even my own people to my rescue.

At this moment I heard a sound on the other side of my palanquin, as if some heavy object had fallen from one of the trees. I opened the door on that side, and peeped out. Before me was a tall, dark-visaged man. As I gazed, horrified, another and yet another man jumped from the branches above me. Four of them picked up the palanquin, placed the poles on their shoulders, and started to run.

Seeing that, my stalwart guardians shouted "Who is that?" and emerging from the water, ran in pursuit. Then it was that I knew I had fallen into the hands of robbers. What was the use of maidenly modesty now? I threw both doors of my palanquin wide open. I saw that my people were running with angry shouts after my captors. At first I had some hopes of a rescue, but these hopes were soon dissipated; for, as we proceeded, more and more robbers sprang from the trees. I have already told you that the lake was surrounded by dense masses of trees, and it was through these that my captors took their way, and were joined by fresh forces as they hastened. Some had bamboo staves in their hands, and some had armed themselves with branches from the trees in which they had been lurking.

Seeing so formidable a crowd, my people began to fall behind. In despair I thought to myself, "Shall I jump from the palanquin?" But my bearers ran so fast that a leap was not without peril, and moreover one of the robbers threatened me with his staff and cried, "If you try to get out, I will break your head." So I kept my seat.

One of my attendants succeeded in catching us up, and laid hold of my conveyance. Alas, one of the robbers smote him on the head, so that he fell senseless on the ground. I did not see him rise again. My belief is that he never rose again.

Seeing this, the others desisted from pursuit, and my captors bore me off without further impediment. They continued their flight uninterruptedly till long after night-fall, and then deposited the palanquin on the ground. I looked round me, and saw dense forest. It was intensely dark. One of the robbers lighted a torch. I was told to give up all I had on pain of instantaneous death. I handed over my jewels and ornaments, taking off even those I had on my person. I was given a coarse, dirty, and torn raiment, which I was compelled to exchange for the pretty dress I wore. When they had thus stripped me, the robbers broke up the palanquin, and tore off its silver ornaments. They then lighted a fire and burned the wood-work, so as to leave no traces of their wicked deed. Then they prepared to depart, leaving me at the mercy of beasts of prey in the gloom of the jungle, far from all human help and habitation. I cried aloud in fear. "I fall at your feet", I said, "I entreat you to take me with you!" I was reduced to such extremity as to desire the company of these reckless and wicked men!

One of the elders among them said to me, not unkindly, "My dear, what are we to do with such a lovely young maiden? The fame of our exploit will soon be all over the countryside, and if we are seen in the company of such as you, we shall be caught."

One of the younger men said, "I am willing to go to prison for so charming a piece of goods. I cannot give her up." I blush now to think of the other odious things he said; I cannot write them down. The older man was, it seems, the leader of the gang. He raised his staff and said, "I will break your head, scoundrel, if you talk thus. Are such sins for the like of us?" So saying, he departed with his followers. As long as I could hear their voices, I retained consciousness. When I could hear them no more, I fell into a dead faint.

II.

I suppose I must have slept, for when I came to my senses the crows and kokilas were already awake and noisy. The light of dawn was shining through the delicate leaves of the bamboo clumps. I rose to my feet and started in search of a village, and after a time came upon human habitations. I asked the people I met if they could tell me the way to my father's village or to that where my father-in-law lived. No one knew. Soon I found, that I was safer in the forest than here. In the first place it was painful for me, a maiden bred in the zenana, to speak to males face to face,—and when I did speak to them, they looked at me with a hungry gaze whose meaning I could not misunderstand. Some mocked at me, some made insulting proposals. I resolved in my mind that I would die rather than again enquire of such creatures. As for the women, none of them could give me any information. They too seemed to take me for some strange animal, so amazed were their foolish faces. Only one old woman said, "My dear, who on earth are you? Is it fitting that such a slim and lovely little person should wander about unattended on the public highway? Dear me! Dear me! You come into my house." I followed her without a word. Seeing me perish with hunger, she gave me food. She said she knew Mahespur. I told her that she would be handsomely rewarded if she took me home. But she only stupidly answered that she could not leave her house and family. So I started once more along the road she indicated. I tramped along painfully till dusk, growing more and more fatigued. Meeting a wayfarer, I asked him how far it was to Mahespur. He stood astonished, and after a time asked me whence I had come. I told him the name of the village where the old woman dwelt. He told me that I was going away from my destination; that Mahespur was two days journey distant.

I was beside myself with fear and disappointment. I asked the man where he was going. He told me that he was on his way to the hamlet of Gaurigram hard by. Not knowing what else to do, I followed him. When we reached the village, the man asked me to whose house I was going. I said I knew no one, and would spend the night under a tree.

"Of what caste are you?" he asked.

"I am a Kayastha", I replied

He said, "I am a Brahmin. Come with me. For all your torn and dirty raiment, I can see that you are of good family. Such looks as yours are not found in humble homes."

Ah, beauty, beauty! I was growing tired of these constant allusions to my pretty looks. But the Brahmin was old and of reverend aspect. I followed him.

I spent that night in the Brahmin's house, and was glad of a little repose after two days of terror and agitation. When I arose in the morning, I found that all my limbs ached. My feet were wofully *[sic]* swollen. I had not strength to sit up.

So long as I was in this weak state, I was compelled to stay in the Brahmin's house. He and his good wife were very kind to me, but I could not think of any means of arriving at Mahespur. None of the women knew the way, nor was any of them ready to be my guide. Many of the men were willing enough, but I was afraid to go alone with men, nor would the old Brahmin have allowed me to accompany them. He took me aside and said, "These are low fellows. Do not trust them. I dare not tell you what they meditate. I cannot, as a respectable Brahmin, allow you to go with such people." So I desisted. One day, I happened to hear that a gentleman named Krishnadas Basu was going to Calcutta with his family, and thought I had at last found a way of escape. Calcutta was far from my home and that of my father-in-law, it is true, but I had a distant relative who was engaged in business in the capital. I thought that if I could only reach Calcutta, I should have no difficulty in finding my relative, who would certainly send me home; or else I might be able to send word to my father.

I announced my discovery to my host, who strongly approved of my plan. "Krishna Babu," he said, "is well known to me. I will take you to him. He is an elderly man of excellent character."

I was duly taken to Krishna Babu's house. The Brahmin explained that I was a young lady of good birth who had fallen into misfortune and had lost my way. "If you will only take this poor friendless girl to Calcutta, she will have no difficulty in finding her way home." Krishnadas Babu agreed, and admitted me to his women's quarters. Next day I started for Calcutta in the company of the ladies of his family. We had to walk some eight or ten miles to the Ganges, where we took boat.

In due course we reached Calcutta, whither my host was proceeding to perform his devotions at the shrine of Kalighat. He took up his residence in the suburb of Bhawanipur. One day he asked me where my relative dwelt. Was it in Calcutta or at Bhawanipur. I had not the slightest idea! Did I not know his address? I did not know that either. In my simplicity I had imagined that Calcutta was just a big village like our own where all the principal inhabitants were known! I thought it was only necessary to mention a gentleman's name to be told where he lived!

I now found that Calcutta was an endless sea of masonry houses. I could think of no means of discovering my friends. Krishnadas Babu very kindly made enquiries on my behalf, but in a place like Calcutta the investigations of a simple country gentleman were of little avail.

It was Krishnadas Babu's intention to go to Benares after he had finished his pilgrimage to Kalighat. When his devotions were completed, it was time for him to resume his journey with his family. What was I to do? I burst into tears.

My kind friend said, "Look here, listen to me. A friend of mine of the name of Ramram Datta lives hard by in Thanthania. I happened to meet him yesterday. He told me that he was in great distress for want of a cook-maid. It happens that girls of quite respectable families in our country go into service as cooks. He asked me if I could recommend some one. I promised to make enquiries. Now why should not you take this chance? I see no other refuge for you. I must tell frankly that my means do not permit me to take you with us to Benares. Even if you came with us, you would be no better off than you are now. On the other hand, if you stay here, you can continue your search for your relatives."

What could I do but agree? But the thought of the trouble my looks had given me returned to my mind. I had come to think of all male beings as my sworn foes. So I asked,

"How old is Ramram Babu?"

"He is an old man like me."

"Is his wife still alive?" I asked.

He had two wives, I was told.

Were there any other males in his family? was my next question. My host replied that there was one little son, aged ten, by the second marriage. And there was also a blind nephew.

I had no further excuse for refusal. The very next day Krishnadas Babu sent me to Ramram Babu's house. I entered his family as his cook. This was what fate had written on my forehead! Who would have guessed that I was destined to earn my living by cooking and waiting at table!

III.

My first idea was that I should soon be able to save enough out of my wages to be able to go home. But no one seemed to know where Mahespur was, nor did I meet anyone who could tell me how to go there. Myself a life-long denizen of the seclusion of a zenana, I did not even know in what district my home was, or in what direction it lay. How then could anyone else guide me? In such fashion a whole year glided by. Then, all of a sudden, a ray of light shone on my darkness. It was as if I had seen a familiar star in a break in the clouds in the rainy season.

One day Ramram Babu called me to him and said:

"I have asked a very important guest to dine with me to-day. He is my banker, and I owe him money. See that to-day's meal is exceptionally good, otherwise I shall be greatly annoyed."

I did my very best. The dining-room was in the women's apartments, and so I was ordered to wait at table. Only Ramram Babu and his guest sat down to eat.

I had already served the first course when they arrived. Presently I went to serve the second course, a dish of meat. I was of course closely veiled, but when was woman's wit obscured by so trifling a matter as a veil? I managed to take a good look at my master's guest.

I found that he was about thirty years old. He was fair of complexion, and extremely good-looking. It was easy to see that he was the sort of man we women admire. Let me admit that as I stood with the dish of meat in my hand, I had another good look at him. While I was thus gazing at him through my parted veil, he raised his head and perceived that my looks were directed to his face. Our Bengali men say that as a light shines brighter in the darkness, so are a veiled woman's eyes brighter than an unveiled woman's looks. It seemed to me that he too was of this opinion. He smiled faintly, and once more bent over his food. I was the only one who caught his smile. In my confusion, I put all the meat into his plate, and hurried away!

I was half ashamed, half delighted. Let me make the dreadful admission that I was more pleasured than ashamed. This was the first smile that had ever given me such joy—no one had ever smiled at me quite like that before, and all the smiles of all the men in the world seemed like poison in comparison.

And now I am sure that all my lady readers who love their lords will frown and say, "Shameless one, but this is falling in love!" It is perfectly true, I had fallen in love. But reflect. Though I was a married woman, I had been practically widowed all my life. I had only seen my husband once at our marriage, and I was then only ten years old. All the desires of my youth were unsatisfied. When the net was thrown into such deep and unplumbed water, what wonder that it raised a big wave!

I must admit that in making this confession, I cannot be acquitted of blame. Whatever its cause, or even if there be no cause, sin is sin. A mere pleading of motives is no excuse for sin. But in all my life this was my first sin—and my last sin—of that kind.

When I returned to my kitchen, the thought came into my mind, "I have seen him before somewhere." To dissipate my doubts, I again went and secretly looked at him. I looked at him attentively, and then I knew!

At this moment, Ramram Babu called to me to bring in a fresh course. I had prepared many dishes. I took one of them into the dining-room. I could see that the guest had not forgotten the look he had intercepted. He said to Ramram Babu, "Ram Babu, tell your cook-maid that her cooking is excellent."

Ram Babu did not understand the secret meaning of this speech. He merely observed, "Yes, she does not cook badly."

But I understood, and mentally resolved that he should know what a clever cook could do to disturb a young man's fancies.

The guest went on, "What surprises me is that one or two of the dishes remind me of the way they cook in our country!"

Again I thought, "it is he!" As a matter of fact I had cooked one or two of the dishes according to the recipes of our quarter of Bengal. Ramram said: "May be, may be, the girl is not from this part of the world."

The guest seized the opportunity, and looking me boldly in the face, he asked, "Where is your home, my girl?"

I thought to myself, shall I tell him, or shall I not? Finally I decided that I would tell him.

But another doubt arose, should I tell him the truth or a lie? I decided that I would tell him a lie. Why I came to this decision, He alone knows who has made the mind of woman deceitful beyond understanding and fond of crooked ways. I thought that if need be, I could tell the truth at any time. Let me deceive him for the present. So it was that I replied:

"Our home is at Kaladighi!"

He was visibly startled. After a time he asked in a gentle voice, "Which Kaladighi? You don't mean Kaladighi of the Dacoits?"

I blush to say I answered, "Yes".

He did not utter another word.

All this time I was standing with the dish in my hand. I had quite forgotten that it was very unbecoming conduct in a Hindu cook-maid to remain standing thus in the presence of men. I noticed that he was no longer enjoying his food. Ramram Babu too observed this and asked:

"Upendra Babu, you are not eating?"

This was all that I was waiting to hear. Upendra Babu! Even before I had heard the name, I knew he was my husband.

I ran into the kitchen, and throwing down the dish, seated myself in sheer ecstasy of joy. Ramram Babu called out, "What was that which fell?" It was merely a dish of meat, after all!

IV.

What am I to do now? From this time forth I must make mention of my husband's name a hundred times in my narrative. Will my lively lady readers kindly sit in committee and tell me what word to use when I make mention of him? Shall I offend their delicate ears by saying "my husband...my husband" over and over again? Or shall I in modern fashion speak of him boldly as "Upendra." Or again, shall I ring poetical changes in a continuous kyrielle of "my lord," "my master," "my dear spouse"? Alas, in the speech of our unfortunate country there is no word by which we can address the one being whom we love to call by name, the one person of whom a loving woman must always be talking! One of my friends (she has had some tincture of town breeding) used to call her husband "Babu." But merely "Babu" seemed a dry mode of address, so she took to calling him "Baburam!"[1] I have half a mind to follow her example!

Well, I have told you how I threw down the dish of food. As I did so, I thought to myself, "since it has pleased destiny to restore me my lost treasure, I must not lose it in another fit of feminine modesty." With this determination, I went and stood in such a place that if any one looked carefully about him when he left the inner apartments, he could not fail to see me. I said to myself, "if he departs without looking about for another glimpse of me, then at the mature age of twenty, I do not know anything about the male sex." I will tell you the plain truth—

and you must try to forgive me. I threw off my veil, and stood shamelessly with bared face. I am ashamed to write it now, but reflect in what trouble of mind I was then!

First of all Ramram passed out. He of course looked straight in front of him, and did not notice me. Then came my husband. My heart throbbed when I saw that he was looking about him—as if he was searching for some one. His eyes fell on me. Of course I knew for whom he was looking. As soon as I caught his eye—how shall I say it? I am covered with confusion. But as it is the cobra's habit to expand his hood before he strikes, so it is with a woman's glance. And why should I not put a little extra poison into my look, seeing that I knew that he was really and truly my "lord and master?" I rather think that the poor man departed badly wounded.

Ramram Babu had another servant girl of the name of Harani. We were great friends. Why not? After all, we were both companions in service. I called her to me and said, "My dear, if you would win my eternal gratitude, find out for me quickly when that babu means to take his departure." Harani laughed and said, "Fie, *didi thakrum[sic]*. I did not know that you had *that* little infirmity!" I laughed too. "It is a long lane," I said, "that has no turning, and every dog must have his day! Now spare me your sermonizing and tell me whether you will help me or not. I assure you there is nothing wrong in the affair, as you will know later." She answered, "Well, I will do it for you; but remember, I would not do this for anyone else."

So, alas, ended poor Harani's attempt at moral instruction!

She departed on her errand and it seemed to my impatience that she was a very long time in returning. I was wriggling, it seems to me, like a fish on dry land. At last Harani came back and announced with a laugh:

"The Babu is not very well, he is going to lie down for a little, I have come for bedding for him."

I answered, "That is all very well, but suppose he goes away in the afternoon! You get hold of him quietly and tell him that our cook says that she is ashamed of her mid-day performance, and begs him to stay for the evening meal. But mind you don't let any one else know of the cook's invitation. You'll see, he will find some pretext to stay longer."

Harani laughed and again said, "Fie, for shame!" But she carried my message nevertheless. In the afternoon she came back to me and said, "I told him what you said. The Babu is a bad man, he agreed to stay."

On hearing this, I was pleased, to be sure. All the same I was a little ashamed of him. It seemed to me that there was no harm in doing what I had done, because I knew who he was. But there was not the remotest possibility that he had recognised me. I had seen him before when he was a full-grown man, and so had my suspicions from the first. He had seen me only as a little girl of eleven. I had not the smallest reason to suppose that he knew me. So it was that I felt aggrieved that, believing me to be another man's wife, he had yielded to the attraction he felt for me. Still he was my husband, I was his wife. It was not for me to think evil of him. So I banished these thoughts from my mind. I merely determined that if, someday, I could recover him, I should cure him of this wicked weakness!

He had not to make long search for an excuse for staying with us. He had recently extended his business operations to Calcutta and had to visit the capital from time to time. His friendship with my master had its origin in business matters. After consenting to Harani's naughty suggestion, he went to Ramram Babu and said, "As I am here, would it not be a good thing if we went into those accounts?" Ramram replied, "By all means, but the ledgers and books are all at my office, let me send for them. It will be nightfall by the time they come. Could you look in to-morrow morning? Or, better still, why not spend the night here?"

To which he replied: "You are very kind. Why stand on ceremony? My friend's house is my house. Let us go into the accounts to-morrow morning."

V.

In the depth of night, when everybody had supped and retired to rest, I stole silently into my master's guest-chamber, of which my husband was the sole occupant.

Remember, this was my first interview with my husband since I had come to woman's estate. How shall I tell you of the queer mixture of pride and shame I felt? I am a sad chatter-box, but when I first addressed him, the words would not come, somehow. I felt as if I dared not speak. I began to tremble in every limb. I could hear my heart beating. My tongue was parched in my mouth. Failing speech, what must I do but fall to crying!

The stupid man, he misunderstood my silly tears! Guess what he said. He said:

"Why are you crying? I did not send for you. You have come of your own accord, and now you cry!"

The cruel speech caused me horrible pain. He considered me a shameless wretch, a suppliant for his favours! My tears flowed afresh at the thought. For a moment I resolved to tell him at once. I could not bear the pain of his scorn. But again it occurred to me that if I told him, he might not believe me. I had told him that my home was at Kaladighi. He would guess that I had heard of his wife's adventure, and was impersonating her for mercenary motives. If some such suspicion were to cross his mind, how was I to convince him? So I resolved to keep my counsel for the present. I sighed, I wiped my eyes, I tried to engage him in conversation. After idle talk on different matters, he said:

"I was much surprised to hear you say that your home is at Kaladighi. I should never have dreamed that such a delightful little person could be born in such a place. I find it difficult to believe, even now, that such a charming girl comes from our rough countryside."

This gave my woman's wits the opportunity for which I was waiting. "You are pleased to flatter a poor servant," I said, "but every one in our country knows that it was your wife who was our reigning beauty. Tell me, sir, have you any news of her?"

"No," he replied coldly, "how long is it since you left home?"

I replied, "it was soon after your wife was carried off that I came here. I suppose, sir, you have married again?"

The answer, to my relief, was "No."

Yes, I was very glad to hear that he had not taken another wife to himself. What I said was, "Of course with such big people as you, a second marriage is a serious matter. If you were to recover your first wife, there might be trouble between the two ladies."

The wretch laughed carelessly and said, "No fear of that, my dear! Supposing she were to turn up, I should not take her back. Think of the scandal! What has become of her caste all this while?"

It was like a thunderbolt! All my hopes were shattered in an instant. What, even if I had revealed myself to him, he would not have accepted me as his wife! Was my growing regard for the creature to be squandered by his cruel words?

I had the courage to ask nevertheless, "If you should meet her now, what would you do?"

He said, with a resolute air, "I should refuse to have anything to do with her."

The heartless wretch! I stood transfixed to stone! I was sick and giddy with disappointment and disgust!

And as I sat there, at the bedside of my dear, dear husband, I said to myself, "Either you shall take me to your arms, my own, my own, or else I shall die as Hindu widows die!"

VI.

And then I banished care from my face. I knew already that it was my smiling glance that had attracted his roving fancy. I thought to myself that if the rhinoceros does not sin in using his mighty horn, if the elephant is permitted to use his tusks, if the tiger defends himself with his cruel claws, if the buffalo can gore his foe with his huge horns, surely a poor little woman may use the feeble weapons at her disposal. "My darling," I thought, "I will use the powers Providence has given me—for your happiness and mine." I left his side and sat down at a distance. I began to converse gaily. He approached me. "Go away," I said, "I see you have made a mistake. You have misunderstood me." I smiled as I spoke, and (I must tell the whole truth, if you are to understand my story) I managed to shake down the braids of my hair. As I talked to him, I occupied myself in binding the coils afresh.

"You have completely misunderstood me," I repeated. "I am no wanton. I merely came to you because I wanted to hear news of home. It is so long since I have met anyone from our country!"

I suppose he did not believe me. He had the audacity to come and sit by me. I only laughed and said, "As you won't obey orders, I must go away. I must say good-night."

So saying, I rose to my feet. Seeing that I was in earnest, the poor man was in despair. He seized my hand. I angrily tore it from his grasp. But still I smiled, I smiled.

And yet I cried, "You are a bad man! Do not touch me! Do you think I am a wanton woman?"

As I spoke, I walked resolutely towards the door. My husband—I am ashamed to use the word as I think of it—restrained me by force.

"Have pity on me," he cried, "have pity on me! Do not go away. I am maddened by the sight of your beauty. Never have I seen such charm, such loveliness!"

I turned back, but I refused to sit down again.

"Ah, Sir," I said, "you have me at a cruel disadvantage. I admit, yes, I admit I like you. Think what it costs me to say no to you! But what can I do? A woman's sole treasure is her virtue. Shall I buy one day's joy with life-long sorrow and shame? Let me go."

"Let me swear," he cried, "that you shall be my heart's mistress all my life long. Why talk of one day's pleasure?"

I laughed, and said I put no faith in such vows. I was going away again and had reached the door, when, no longer able to restrain himself, he fell at my feet and held me back.

I was filled with pain to see his evil plight. "Let us go to your lodgings," I said, tempting him. "If we stay here, you will go away presently and leave me."

Of course he was only too ready to consent. His lodging was hard by, in Simla, and we went thither, he and I together. When we got there, I noticed that there were two rooms. Into one of these I preceded him, slammed the door in his face, and drew the bolts! The poor man was left outside!

He made the most piteous entreaties to be admitted. I laughed and said, "I have now entered *your* service. But let me see if the flood of your passion will not have run dry by to-morrow morning. If I find that you are still as fond of me to-morrow, we will have some further talk. Now say good-night, and go away."

I utterly refused to open the door, and finally he went away elsewhere. I hope he slept! It was quite late in the morning when I opened the door. I found him humbly waiting my pleasure. I took his hand in mine.

"Lord and master," I said, "either send me back to Ramram Datta, or promise not to come near me for a whole week. Let that be a test of your patience and fortitude."

My husband agreed to undergo this heroic test.

VII.

Whatever means of inflaming males Providence has entrusted to our sex, these I heartlessly employed in the torture of my husband during his week's trial. How am I, a woman, to describe a woman's arts and wiles? If by right of womanhood I had not known how to kindle the flame, why was there such a blaze in the poor man's heart last night? But by what means I lighted the fire, how cunningly I blew it when it smouldered, how I managed to set my husband's heart aflame, I cannot for sheer shame tell the tale of all this.

If any of my fair readers has ever engaged in the task of man-slaughter, and has succeeded in her endeavour, then she will understand. If any of my male readers has ever suffered at the hands of a destroying angel, I need not tell him of my tactics. Are not we women, in short, the thorns of this weary world? Is it not mere history that the world has suffered more from us women than from all the men that were ever born of women? Luckily our sex is for the most part unaware of its destructive power, else by this time our poor globe would have been destroyed by fire!

During this week of trial I was constantly in my husband's company. I spoke to him affectionately and sympathetically. I carefully abstained from idle gossip. Smiles, and looks, and gestures, are not these the natural arms of our weak sex? The first day, I was condescending and kind. The second day, I showed signs of growing affection. The third day, I took it upon myself to supervise his domestic affairs. I was careful to see that due arrangements were made for his comfort in eating, sleeping, and bathing. Nothing was neglected that contributed to his well-being. I cooked with my own hand; I even cut up the firewood. Climax of shame—one day I wept! I refused to tell him plainly why I was crying. But I let him understand that I dreaded that when the trial was over, his passion might be sated, he might tire of me, and desert me. One day he was not very well. I sat up all night with him and tended him. Do not despise me for all this wicked behaviour. From my heart I say that it was not all cunning and pretences. I was beginning to love him very dearly. Shall I say that I was already almost half as much in love with him as he was in love with me? Need I say that before the week was up, I would not have left him if he had beaten me and tried to drive me away?

Nor need I tell you that fresh fuel was being added to the flame that consumed him. By degrees he abandoned all his other pursuits for the pleasure of being with me. When I was occupied with my house-work, he followed me about like a child. At every step I could see the growing strength of his passion, and yet at a hint from me he would restrain himself. At length he had come to such a pass that he would touch my feet in the Hindu way of showing submission, would entreat me not to leave him when his trial was over. And in truth it seemed to me that I had become so necessary to him that he would lose his senses if I deserted him.

When the last day of the probation came round, I wept and said to him, "Dearest, I did wrong to come with you, I have given you undeserved pain and trouble. It seems to me that this probation has been a foolish mistake. Who can predict the course of a man's passions? You have loved me fondly all these eight days. But eight months hence—can you yourself say whether you will still love me? And if you desert me, think of what my state will be!"

He rose to his feet with a laugh. "If that is your only anxiety," he said, "I can easily put your mind at rest. I had thought of doing it before, but now my mind is made up. I shall make due provision for you."

I had been waiting for a chance of leading him to say something of the sort. I was the more pleased when he said it of his own accord.

"Fie," I cried, "if you leave me, what need shall I have of money? If it is merely a question of living, a woman can live by begging. But I do not wish to live if you leave me. What I want is a proof, my dear, that you will not leave me all my life long. For to-day is the last day of my darling's trial."

"What will you have me do?" he asked, "I will do whatever you desire."

"I am only a woman," I replied, "what shall I say? Think it out for yourself."

Then I led the talk to other subjects. By degrees I fell to telling him a silly story—made up, of course—about a man who had made a deed of gift of all his property to his mistress. That was the gist of it.

He ordered his carriage to be got ready, and drove away. This was the first time he had left me during the whole week. Presently he returned, but did not tell me where he had been, nor did I venture to ask him. In the afternoon, he went out again. When he came back, he had a paper in his hand.

"Take this," he said; "this is a deed giving you the whole of my worldly goods. I got a lawyer to draw it up. If ever I desert you, I shall be driven to begging my bread in the streets!"

This time the tears that came to my eyes were genuine enough. Did my dear love me so dearly as that? I stooped to touch his feet, and said, "From this day forth, I am thy bond-woman, thy bought slave. The probation is ended."

VIII.

Now it was that I could say to myself, "I hold in my hand the moon for which I was crying. How shall he leave me now? He said he would not receive me back as his wife, did he?" The purpose for which I had spread all these nets was accomplished. If I were to tell him now that I was his wife, and he were to abandon me, he would have to give up all his worldly wealth and position.

It was my father who had named me Indira, after Laksmi, the goddess of good fortune. My mother used to call me

Kumudini or "Lily." At my father-in-law's house I was known as Indira; at home nearly everybody called me Kumudini. At Ramram Babu's I had told them that my name was Kumudini, and had half forgotten that I was ever Indira. My husband too knew me by my second name, and it was under this name that I was described in the deed of gift.

Some happy days we spent together in Calcutta. All this time I refrained from announcing myself. I thought I would do so some day when we went to Mahespur. By various roundabout ways, I got my husband to tell me news of home. All was well with my dear ones, but I began to long to see their faces again.

One day I said to my husband, "I want to go to Kaladighi to see my father and mother. Send me home for a while."

He was not at all willing. How was he to exist without me? On the other hand he had become so accustomed to obeying orders that he could not definitely say "no." What he said was, "It will take at least a fortnight for you to go to Kaladighi and return. I shall die of weariness in all that time. I will go with you."

I clapped my hands and said, "That is just what I wanted! But where will you stay in a place like Kaladighi?"

"How long do you want to be at home?" he asked.

"If I cannot see you," I replied, "five days will be the longest time I can stay away from you."

"In that case," he said, "I shall go to my own home for five days. On the fifth day, remember, I shall come and take you away."

This arrrangement having been arrived at, in due course we mounted in our respective palanquins and started on our journey. After we had passed the lake of unhappy memory and were in the village of Kaladighi, my husband left me and wended his way homewards.

When his back was turned, I said to my bearers, "I want to go to Mahespur first. I will come back to Kaladighi afterwards. Take me to Maheshpur. You shall be well paid for your trouble."

They carried me to my native village. Telling the bearers and my other attendants to wait on the outskirts, I entered the village on foot. When my old home came in sight at last, I sat down in a secluded place and shed happy tears. It was long before I could muster courage to enter the house. The first person I met in our old home was my dear father. I fell at his feet in obeisance. He was beside himself with joy when he recognised his long lost daughter. But I will spare you the details of all these happenings. Indeed, how shall I tell of things so sacred, so intimate?

I refused to tell them where I had been and what I had been doing. When my father and mother pressed me, I said, "I will tell you some other time."

The next day, my father sent a letter to my father-in-law's house. To the messenger he said, "if my son-in-law is not at home, find out where he is, and give this letter into his own hands."

I begged my mother not to let anyone know that I had returned. "I have been so long away from home," I said. "If he should be unwilling to receive me back, he may refuse to come. Bring him here on some other pretext. If only you can get him here, trust me to allay his suspicions."

My mother communicated my wishes to my father, who agreed to follow my advice. In his letter he wrote, "I am about to make a will. You are my son-in-law; you are dear to me, and my well-wisher. I want to consult you as to the disposition of my property. Please come here as soon as possible after receipt of this letter."

My husband came immediately, and my father at once told him the whole truth. For a while, my husband remained absorbed in thought. Then he said, "I have the highest regard for you, Sir. Though you have brought me here on a false pretext, I am glad to have had the privilege of seeing you. But your daughter has been absent from home this long time. No one knows where she has been, or what sort of a reputation she has made for herself. Therefore, I regret to say, I cannot admit her to my home."

My father was grievously offended. He reported the matter to my mother, who informed me. I told my companions to tell my parents not to be anxious. "Bring him to me," I said, "into the inner apartments, and trust me to deal with him."

But the obstinate man utterly refused to enter the women's quarters.

"I will not meet a wife," he said, "whom I refuse to take into my house." Finally, moved by the tears of my mother, and the laughter and sarcasms of my young companions, he consented to take a light meal in the inner apartments.

He took his seat in the room prepared for his refection. There was no one standing near him. They had all gone away. He was eating with downcast head, when I crept silently behind him, and suddenly put my hands over his eyes.

He laughed and said, "As if I did know that it was you, Kamini, with your silly baby tricks!"

Kamini was my youngest sister.

I said, "I am not Kamini. Tell me who I am, and I will let you go."

On hearing the sound of my voice, he started, and asked huskily, "Who is it?"

I took away my hands from his eyes, and stood in front of him.

"Chief of deceivers," I said, "my name is Indira. I am the daughter of Hara Mohan Datta, and this my paternal home. My morning reverence to your worship! May I venture to ask after the welfare of your friend Kumudini?"

He was speechless! I could not help noting, however, that he was delighted to see me.

"What practical joke is this, Kumudini," he said, "and, how did you come here?"

"Kumudini is only one of my names," I replied. "What a stupid old thing you are not to have recognised me all this time! Why, I knew you the moment you sat down to eat at Ramram Datta's house! Do you suppose I would have allowed you to talk to me in the way you did otherwise, Sir? My own, my husband, your wife is no wanton."

For a time he was as one dumbfounded. Then he asked, "Why then have you deceived me all this time?"

The reply was easy. "The very first day you saw me, you said to me that if you recovered your wife, you would not take her back; otherwise I would have told you then who I was."

I had tied his deed of gift in my *sari*. I loosed the knot, and showing him the document, I said, "That first night, I resolved that either you would take me back as your true and loving wife, or else I would die. It was in order to carry out that resolve that I induced you to get this paper written. I see now that I did wrongly. If it be my lord's wish, let me come to your home as your wife. If you think me unworthy of so high an honour, let your servant sweep the courtyard of your house, so that at least she may see your dear face sometimes. As for your deed of gift, it has served its purpose." So saying I tore the paper into little bits.

He rose to his feet, he held me in his dear, strong arms. He said to me, "Dearest, you are my all, my own. I cannot live without you. Come, my wife, and be the mistress of your husband's home."

---

1. That is to say, "do not smile at their upstart ways!"
2. Which made the loving title jocular, and even disrespectful.

RADHARANI

I.

A LITTLE girl called Radharani had been to the village of Mahesh in order to witness the exciting ceremony of pulling the Juggernauth car. She was hardly eleven years of age. Time was when her people had been very wealthy, for the child came of a great family in these parts. But when her father died, a relative brought a civil suit against her widowed mother. The suit involved the whole of the family property. The widow lost her case in the Calcutta High Court. No sooner did this happen than the heartless plaintiff executed his decree and ousted her from the family home. The landed property, amounting to some ten lakhs of rupees, all went to the plaintiff. What money there was in hand, was expended in paying costs and law expenses. Radharani's mother sold her jewels and other movable property, and instituted an appeal before the Hon'ble Privy Council in London. But there was nothing left for the maintenance of mother and daughter. The widow found a precarious asylum in a small cottage on the family estate and endeavoured to earn her living by manual labour. She was unable to set aside a dower for her daughter's marriage.

To add to their misfortunes, the mother fell ill, and was no longer able to work for her living. The pair were in danger of starvation. The mother was too ill to need much food, the child often fasted because there was nothing to eat. On the day of the Car Festival the mother's disease reached a critical stage: medicines and nourishment were necessary. But how was the child to procure them?

With tearful eyes Radharani gathered some jungle flowers and wove them into garlands, thinking to sell them at the fair, which was an incident of the Car Festival. She hoped by this means to get a few pice wherewith to buy necessities for her sick mother. But before the ceremony was half over, heavy rain fell and dispersed the crowd. Not a soul bought the girl's simple garlands. Radharani stayed on. What matter if she were soaked by the rain? Perhaps the storm would abate and the spectators would return. But, alas, the rain continued pitilessly. No one came back to the deserted car. Evening drew on, and night fell. The night was stormy and dark, and poor Radharani had to turn weeping homewards.

The night was very dark, the roads were miry and slippery, the child had to feel her way through the growing dusk. Added to that, the heavy rain of the month of Sravan fell on her with a force that made her cower before the storm. Worst and most cruel of all was the thought that she had been unable to make any provision for her mother's needs. Half blinded by her tears, by the storm, by the darkness of the night, the child felt her way, stumbling and falling. The wet locks of her loose hair were blown across her rainwashed face. But the child clung pathetically to the paltry garlands she had woven, and held them tight to her bosom.

As she was struggling bravely along, someone emerged from the darkness and ran up against the child. So far Radharani had not wept audibly. The shock and surprise overcame her childish resolution, and for the first time she could not restrain a piteous wail.

The newcomer asked, kindly enough, "Who is this small person crying in the dark?" It was a man's rough voice, but there was something in its tone that stayed the child's tears. The voice was that of a stranger, but the girl felt instinctively that it expressed kindness and compassion. She stopped crying and said:

"We are very poor people. There is no one now but mother and me."

The man asked, "And where have you been wandering, my little maid?"

"I went to see the Car Festival. I was on my way home. But in the rain and wet I have lost my way."

"And where, pray, *is* your home?"

"We live at Srirampur", said Radharani.

"That is all right", said the man. "As it happens, I was going to Srirampur myself. Come along with me. You shall tell me as we go in what part of the village you live, and I will see you safely home. Dear me, it is very slippery, isn't it? Here, give me your hand, and then we can hold one another up!"

In such fashion the pair struggled along together. In the darkness it was impossible for Radharani's new friend to know her age, but he guessed from her childish voice and words that she was very young. However he took occasion to ask, "And how old may you be, little maiden?"

"I am between ten and eleven."

"And what is your name?"

"My name is Radharani."

"Well, my friend Radharani, I should like very much to know what induced a young person of your age to tramp off all alone to a Car Festival in a strange village? I am not sure that you are a very prudent young girl."

By degrees, word by word, with kindly and humorous questions, he induced the child to tell him the story of the garlands, and of her disappointed hopes of earning money for her mother. He learned that it was not really to see the Car Festival that our little maiden had gone to Mahesh, but to sell her poor little garlands so as to buy necessaries for her sick mother. And she had not been able to sell her garlands. She was hugging them to her bosom now.

"Well", he said, "this is a wonderful thing. I was just looking for just such a garland for our family idol. The fair broke up so suddenly that I could not buy what I wanted. Will you sell me one of your garlands?"

Radharani was hugely pleased. But, she thought, how can I ask a price of a stranger who has come to my aid so kindly and generously? And again the thought came, "But if I don't, what is poor mother to do for the food she needs?"

With these confused thoughts in her mind, the child handed one of the garlands to her companion.

"Let me see now", he said, "the proper price of this will be four pice. Here is the money all ready."

So saying he handed her some money. Radharani said, "But are these pice? The coins seem very big."

"Little goose, can't you see that I have only given you two? They are *double* pice."

"But they look very bright, even in the darkness. Are you sure you have not given me rupees by mistake?"

"Not a bit of it. They are new coins, fresh from the mint. That is why they shine so."

"Never mind", said Radharani. "I will light a lamp when we get home, and if you have made a mistake, I will give you back your money. Only you will have to wait a little till I have lighted the lamp, you know."

Presently they reached the cottage where Radharani's mother dwelt. The girl turned to the stranger: "You must please come in and wait while we light a lamp and see whether these are silver rupees or not."

"No", said her companion. "I will wait outside. You go in and change your wet clothes, and then see about getting a light."

Radharani replied, "But I have got no change of clothes at all. My other *sari* has gone to the washerman. So, you see, I am accustomed to sitting in wet clothes. It does not do me any harm. I will wring out the skirt presently. Now, will you wait a moment while I strike a light?"

There was no oil in the house, so the girl was forced to take a handful of straw from the thatch. This she lighted with flint and steel. All this took some time. When she had procured a light, Radharani saw that she had indeed two rupees in her hand. She ran out, improvised torch in hand. She searched everywhere. The stranger was gone!

Radharani was in despair. She told the whole tale to her mother, and, gazing anxiously in her face, exclaimed, "What are we to do now?"

The mother replied, "What can we do, my child? I cannot believe that he gave the money by mistake. Doubtless he is a generous gentleman, who took pity on us when he heard our story. We are but beggar folk now, my daughter. We must accept the gift without false shame."

While mother and daughter were talking thus, someone suddenly knocked at the door and put them in great confusion. Radharani ran to open the door, thinking that her friend had doubtless returned to claim his money. Alas, it was nothing of the sort. To the girl's dismay, she found only the village draper standing in the doorway.

The cottage was not very far from the bazaar, one of the nearest shops in which was that of Padma Lochan, the draper. It was that worthy tradesman in person who now stood at the door, bearing a lovely pair of newly woven *saris* from Santipore, which he put into the girl's hands.

"These", he said, "are for Radharani."

Radharani exclaimed, "There must be some mistake! How can these be for me?"

Padma Lochan—who may or may not have deserved the mental disapproval with which the disappointed girl received him—seemed surprised at her question.

"All I know," he replied, "is that a Babu paid for them in hard cash and ordered me to bring them to you."

Radharani exclaimed, "It is he, I am sure it is he! He has bought the cloth and sent it to me. Tell me, Padma Lochan."

I ought to stop here to explain that the worthy cloth-merchant had known the family in the days of their prosperity. On the occasion of Hindu festivals, when it is the custom to make presents of cloth to friends and dependants, often and often had he sold them four rupees worth of cloth at its proper price (on his solemn word of honour) of eight rupees twelve annas and odd pice, and had merely made two annas profit on the transaction! "Tell me, Padma Lochan", the girl said, "do you know the Babu of whom you speak?"

Padma Lochan replied, "What, do you not know him yourself?"

The girl replied, "No."

"Well, I thought he was some relation of yours. I do not know him."

Be that as it may, friend Padma Lochan had once more sold four rupees worth of cloth for eight rupees fourteen annas (including profit), and seeing no need of further discussion, the honest vender departed to his shop with a sense of virtue rewarded.

Meanwhile Radharani herself ran to the bazaar, and changing the rupees, purchased what she required for her mother's needs. She brought home oil, and lighted the lamp. She did the simple cooking required for her mother's simple invalid fare. Before bringing the food to the bedside, she set to work, in the Hindu fashion, of preparing for a meal, to sweep the room. While she was thus engaged, she picked up a piece of paper. Running to her mother with it, she asked, "What is this, mother?"

Her mother examined the paper and exclaimed, "Why, this is a currency note!"

"Then in that case *he* must have thrown it in through the door."

"Yes, he meant it for a present for you. Besides, look what is written on it. 'For Radharani'."

Radharani said, "Oh, how good of him! Did you ever hear of such a kind person before, mother?"

Her mother replied, "Look, he has written his name on the note, too. Do you know why he has done that? Because people might refuse to change it for fear it was stolen. His name is Rukmini Kumar Ray."

Next day mother and daughter made many enquiries as to who Rukmini Kumar Ray might be. But no one seemed to know of any one of that name in Srirampur or any of the adjacent villages. They did not change the note. They put it carefully away. They were very poor, but they were not avaricious.

II.

It was much that Radharani's mother should have got the little comforts she needed. But her infirmity continued to increase. She had been a very wealthy woman. She was now reduced to dire poverty. What with bodily fatigue and mental anxiety her vitality was sapped. Her illness grew steadily worse, and at last it was plain that her end was near.

It was at this time that news came from England that the Lords of the Privy Council had decided the case in her favour. It seemed that she was to get her property back, that the law expenses and costs were to be refunded to her, the heavy costs of three successive trials in court. One Kamakhyanath Babu had been their pleader in the High Court, and this gentleman came in person to their cottage to tell them the news. On hearing this joyful news, the dying woman shed happy tears. Restraining her excitement, however, she said to her lawyer,

"You have brought oil, my friend, to a dying lamp! This good news of yours has come too late to save my life. My days are numbered. But I have this great joy, that my little daughter need not die of starvation when I am gone. And yet, how can I be sure of that? She is but a child, poor dear! Who will defend her rights and her property? In you, my friend, is my only hope. Grant a dying woman her last request. Promise to be a father and guardian to my child."

Kamakhyanath Babu was not only the kindest but most trustworthy of men, and an old friend of Radharani's father. When misfortune befell the family, he had begged Radharani's mother to take up her abode with him till the appeal was decided. In Hindu phrase, he offered to make her his adopted mother. But the old lady was too proud to accept her lawyer's hospitality. Finally the good man was driven to offer a monthly subvention to their needs, but his client heroically declared that she had enough money in hand for present needs, and would come to him if she were in real need. The gift they had accepted from Rukmini Kumar was the first and last charity they had received from anyone! Hence it was that their lawyer was unaware to what straits they had been reduced. When he found them in abject poverty, he was much vexed and grieved. He was greatly moved when his client, once more made a fresh prayer of him with joined palms of entreaty.

"Madam," he said, "you have only to order, it is for me to carry out your instructions. I will faithfully attend to all your lightest wishes."

"The time is come for me to depart," she said, "and I leave my girl behind me. The courts have now confirmed my father-in-law's genuine will, and Radharani is heiress to a great estate. I beseech you to have care of her; treat her as your daughter; protect her from those who prey on the wealthy. This is my dying request to you. If you will promise me this, my friend, I can die in peace."

Her lawyer replied, "I swear to you by all that is holy that Radharani shall be to me more than a daughter. I promise this with all my heart, and you may trust to me to do my duty by my young ward."

The dying woman looked at him, and seeing the tears in his eyes, gladly accepted his assurance. A flickering smile of pleasure shone for a moment on her parched and fevered lips. This smile told the experienced lawyer that the poor woman knew that she was doomed. Kamakhya Babu now renewed his entreaties to his client to take up her abode under his roof. She might move to her old home, he said, when the legal formalities had been concluded. Her old pride and reluctance to accept obligations were due to poverty. While she was still poor, she was too proud to accept the hospitality of richer people. Now that she was restored to riches, her fierce independence had disappeared. She very gently and kindly accepted her old friend's offer, and the lawyer with the utmost care and tenderness conveyed the sick woman and her daughter to his home.

All that medical skill could do was attempted in vain, and the widow died very shortly after the restoration of her fortunes. Radharani's lawyer took the necessary steps to have the heiress put in possession of her property. But seeing that she was but a child still, he retained her as his guest and did not send her to her ancestral home. The Collector of the district, who in India takes the place of the Court of Chancery, was desirous of putting the estate under the Court of Wards, but Kamakhya Babu was of opinion that he would be a better guardian of the girl's interests than any government official. His legal astuteness defeated the Collector's well-meant plans and he found himself free to defend his ward's interests without official interference. His most serious responsibility was the need of finding a suitable husband for the heiress. Fortunately the good lawyer was a man of modern ideas and no advocate of infant marriages. He reflected, too, that the girl had no old-fashioned relatives who would imagine that her caste was in danger if she were not married in childhood. He made up his mind, therefore, that the question might be shelved till Radharani herself began to think about a husband. In the meanwhile let her have a suitably liberal education. Holding these opinions, the excellent man made no effort whatever to find a husband for his ward, but devoted all his efforts to securing her the best teachers.

III.

Five years have elapsed, and Radharani is now an extremely comely young woman of sixteen. But she is carefully confined to the feminine apartments. No male has seen her budding charms. Yet, even to the most advanced minds, the time has come to settle upon an alliance for the lovely young heiress. Her guardian was of opinion that the girl's own wishes should be consulted. In order to sound his ward, the lawyer sent for his own daughter, Vasanta Kumari, who had long been Radharani's friend and playmate. The two girls were of the same age and devotedly attached to one another. Kamakhya Babu directed Vasanta to sound her friend on the subject that now began to give him no little anxiety. Vasanta, somewhat bashfully, but with a merry smile on her lips, asked her father,

"Is there such a person as Rukmini Kumar Ray?"

Kamakhya Babu was puzzled, and said, "No, not that I know of. Why do you ask?"

Vasanta answered, "Because Radharani will not marry anyone except Rukmini Kumar Ray."

The good lawyer was much disturbed.

"What is that you say?" he cried. "How should Radharani make the acquaintance of a young man who is unknown to me?"

Vasanta laughed mischievously. She had repeatedly heard the story of the adventure on the way home from the Car Festival, and told the tale at length to her father, who was much impressed by the delicate generosity of the unknown Rukmini Kumar.

"But tell her from me, my girl," he added, "that she has fallen into a deplorable error. Tell her that marriage is not a matter of gratitude. It is right and proper, I admit, that she should be grateful to this generous stranger, and if time and occasion serve, it is fitting that she should show her gratitude in some suitable fashion. But to give herself in marriage to him is a different thing altogether. We know neither his caste nor his condition, his age nor his means. In all probability he is a married man with a family. What likelihood is there, then, that he will be in a position to marry Radharani?"

"Well, but, father," answered Vasanta, "Radharani knows all this just as well as you and I do. But ever since that night the girl has made for herself a mental image of her protector and has set it up in her heart. As others do daily worship to their family gods, so Radharani daily worships her idol. During the five years that she has been under our roof, I doubt if a single day has gone by without her mentioning him to me. If you marry her to anyone else, I promise you that her husband will not be a happy man."

"Dear me, dear me," thought the lawyer, "this is the green sickness of a romantic maid, a case calling for medicine. But the first medicine, it seems to me, is to find the mysterious Rukmini Kumar."

Accordingly the good man set to work to find the generous stranger. He made personal enquiries himself. He set his friends to work to search on his behalf. He wrote innumerable letters to all his many clients all over the country. He inserted an advertisement in all the newspapers. The advertisement was thus worded:

'Will Babu Rukmini Kumar Ray kindly arrange for an interview with the undersigned on a matter of much importance? The undersigned begs to assure him that the result is likely to be to his advantage.'

But all these energetic measures were of no avail. Days, months, nay, years, slipped by and Rukmini Kumar still remained a mystery. Then Radharani suffered another grievous bereavement. Her kind friend and guardian also died. This loss caused her the deepest grief. She felt herself to be orphaned a second time. After the funeral and attendant ceremonies were over, she took up her abode in her family home, and assumed the personal charge of the responsibilities of her estate, which had much increased under Kamakyha Babu's watchful and intelligent care.

Immediately after her estate came into her own hands, the young heiress made over two lakhs of rupees to the government, with the request that an asylum and hospital for poor and needy people should be founded in her native village, to be known as "The Rukmini Kumar Prasad" or Benefaction.

The government officials were somewhat surprised at the proposed title, but that was of course the generous donor's business. The asylum was duly constructed and inaugurated. In the time of her poverty, her mother had left her own village and had built her little cottage at the distant village of Srirampar *[sic]*. Why? Because she felt that it would be painful, in her poverty, to live in the place where she had been prosperous and happy. Their ancestral home was in a village which I shall take the liberty of calling Rajpur, lest I should give a clue to the identity of my heroine. It was in Rajpur in face of her own dwelling, that Radharani commemorated her sufferings and gratitude by erecting the poor-house, which was speedily filled with the needy and unfortunate from many miles around.

IV.

One or two years after this, a gentleman made his appearance at Radharani's poor-house. He was about thirty-five or thirty-six years old. He was of grave but kindly appearance, and seemed to be in comfortable circumstances. He stood for some time in the gateway of the Rukmini Kumar Prasad and finally asked the attendants whose residence it was. He was told that it was not a private dwelling, but an asylum for the poor and indigent. He was also informed of the name it bore. He asked if he might visit the institution.

"Why," they replied, "should not such an one as you enter a building which is open to all the poor and miserable of the land?"

The stranger made a careful inspection of the asylum, and returning to the entrance, said,

"I have carefully examined all the arrangements for the comfort of the poor and sick, and am greatly pleased. To whose generosity do we owe this institution? Is his name Rukmini Kumar?"

The attendants replied, "No, sir, this institution has been founded by our mistress, Srimati Radharani Dasi."

"Why, then," asked the stranger, "is it called the Rukmini Kumar Benefaction?"

The attendants said that they did not know.

"Who then is this Rukmini Kumar?"

"No one of whom we know."

"Where is the residence of the generous foundress?"

The attendants pointed out a handsome mansion hard by.

"Can you tell me," said the stranger, "is the lady married or a widow?"

"She is neither married nor a widow. She comes of great people. All her relatives are dead. There is no one to give her in marriage."

"Does the lady ever admit male visitors to an interview? Do not be offended at my question. Let me tell you that many Hindu ladies now go into mixed society like Englishwomen. That is why I ask."

"Indeed," the attendants indignantly replied, "our lady has no such foreign manners. She never shows herself to males, even if they be friends of the family."

The stranger walked thoughtfully away towards the heiress's residence and entered its hospitable gate.

V.

Our new friend was attired much in the fashion of an ordinary Bengali gentleman. If he was well and carefully dressed, there was nothing conspicuous about his costume, save that he wore a flashing diamond in a ring. So large and handsome was the stone that it even attracted the attention of the doorkeepers, who had never seen so magnificent a jewel before. Nevertheless he was alone and unattended, and they began asking themselves who the stranger might be. They waited for him to announce himself, but he seemed calmly oblivious of the necessity of doing so. He asked to be taken to Radharani's head bailiff and handed a letter to that dignitary, saying, "Be good enough to give this letter to your mistress, and bring me her answer."

The bailiff respectfully replied, "Sir, my mistress is an unmarried lady and still young. She has therefore made a rule that if any letter comes addressed to her by an unknown person, we are to read it before transmitting it to her."

The stranger calmly replied, "Very well, read it then."

The bailiff read as follows:—

Dear Sister,

Though the bearer of this letter is a male, admit him to a private interview. Have no fear. And mind you write and tell me what passes between you!

Your old friend,
SRIMATI VASANTA KUMARI.

On seeing the well known signature of Kamakhya Babu's daughter, no one raised any further objection. The letter was taken into the inner apartments.

Presently a maid-servant came to escort the stranger to the ladies' quarters. No male was to accompany him. Such were her mistress's orders.

The maid ushered the visitor into a handsomely furnished apartment. This was the first time a man had ever penetrated into the fair Radharani's private apartments. At sight of him, one maid departed to inform her mistress. Another stayed, and after the manner of her kind, made a careful inventory of the visitor's appearance. His complexion, she noted, was fair, fair as the *mallika* flower in full bloom. His stature was tall, his form muscular and sturdy. His forehead was lofty, surmounted by curling locks of the deepest black. His eyes were large and frank. The eyebrows were clearly pencilled, bushy, and as black as the hair on his head. His nose was straight and of an aristocratic fineness of outline. His lips were red and not excessively full; his neck was long, but strong and muscular. His limbs were hidden by his cloak, but the maid could see that his hands were finely shaped, and that on one of the tapering fingers was a splendid diamond.

Radharani dismissed her attendant as she entered the room. The sight of the lovely girl who approached him thrilled him as if a new sun had arisen in his life. His whole person seemed irradiated with her fresh loveliness. It was his place to speak first, seeing that he was a male and the elder of the two, but he was so entranced by the girl's beauty that he was speechless. Radharani showed some annoyance at his silence and said,

"Will you kindly explain why you have asked for a private interview with me? I am, as you know, an unmarried woman, and if I have acceded to your request, it was only at Vasanta's entreaty."

The visitor said, "Yet I cannot say that I was exactly eager for the great privilege of being admitted to your presence!"

Radharani was still more offended.

"Is that so?" she replied. "You will note that my friend has offered no explanation of the reasons for asking me to see you. Perhaps you can inform me."

The visitor produced a very old and tattered newspaper and handed it to Radharani, who saw that it contained Kamakhya Babu's advertisement for the long sought Rukmini Kumar. As she looked at it, the girl trembled like a palm tree in a storm. As she examined the stranger's comely form, she asked herself, could this be the benefactor of her childhood? Curiosity overcame her maidenly modesty, and it was in an eager voice that she asked,

"Are you, sir, by any chance Rukmini Kumar Babu?"

The stranger replied, "Madam, no!"

On hearing this unexpected reply, the girl moved slowly to a seat. She felt unable to continue standing—she was the prey of surprising, of conflicting emotions.

"No," the visitor repeated, "if I had been Rukmini Kumar, your guardian would not have issued this advertisement, for I was well known to him. But when I saw it in the newspaper, I carefully put it aside for future use."

"If, Sir," said the heiress, "this advertisement has no reference to you, why did you preserve it, may I ask?"

"Why? For a joke, I think. Some eight or ten years ago, it was my whim to wander about on foot in search of foolish adventures. I was afraid of becoming the laughing stock of my friends in a country where such random travels are scarcely considered respectable, and so I assumed the fictitious name of Rukmini Kumar. Why do you look so astonished?"

Radharani, with an effort, resumed some show of composure.

The stranger continued, "I do not, as it happens, know anyone who is legally entitled to the name. It seemed to me in the highest degree improbable that anyone was making search for me. However, one never knows. On second thoughts I laid the paper aside in a safe place, but I never had the audacity to question Kamakhya Babu on the subject."

"And then?"

"And then, when your guardian died, his sons invited me to the funeral, but business engagements prevented me from accepting the invitation. When I returned home, my natural desire was to see them and beg them to excuse my absence on such an occasion. Half in fun, I brought the advertisement with me. In the course of conversation I contrived to ask Kamakhya Babu's eldest son how this advertisement came to be issued. He replied that it was by the orders of Radharani. Now I too had met a girl called Radharani, and though I only saw her once, I had been unable to dismiss her from my thoughts. The child, though she was half starving herself, had woven garlands of jungle flowers to buy necessities for her sick mother. She was struggling home in her disappointment through pouring rain and blinding darkness. Poor little soul! The thought of her distress still affects me."

The speaker's voice betrayed emotion. Radharani swallowed the tears that would rise. Bravely, however, she said,

"Why all this talk about a wretched little girl? Will you kindly explain your own business with *me*?"

"Ah madam," he answered, "do not speak thus harshly of the child. If ever there was a sweet little maid in this world, it was my little wayside acquaintance. If ever in my wanderings I met a maiden who had in her the makings of a gracious and noble lady, it was my little friend Radharani. If ever there was, in our Hindu phrase, ambrosia on a woman's lips, I found it in the artless prattle of my girlish acquaintance. Ah, madam, you may laugh, but you have read in our poets of the instruments on which the heavenly apsaras play for the beguiling of poor mortals. I know not how it was, but the child's words, simple yet crystal clear in their utterance, reminded me of what the poets say of the fascination of the heavenly singers. For all her simplicity, no woman's voice has so affected me or sunk so deeply into my memory."

And Rukmini Kumar (for so we must now call him) said to himself, "Such too is the ravishing voice I hear to-day." It was years since he had heard the girl's broken speech and yet he recognised it in the polished tones of the beautiful woman before him. It was as if it were only yesterday. And yet, he thought, is it the same Radharani? What a fool I am! That was a poor little frightened beggar maid dwelling in a thatched cottage, and this is the lovely heiress of great possessions. I barely saw the little maid whose voice lingers in my memory. I do not even know whether she was ugly or pretty, and yet...... yet if this beautiful being has only a tithe of that little maid's charm, what a woman for a man to love and waste his life on!

Radharani, on the other hand, drank in the stranger's courteous words. A strange and happy emotion filled her maidenly breast. "Ah!" she thought, "all these pretty things you say about your little friend of yore, it is to you, sir, they should be addressed. And from whence have you come after these eight long years of absence? Have you descended, god-like, from some heavenly paradise? Have you at last been touched by the heart's devotion of your loving servant? Can you be a heavenly being, able to wander unseen into maidens' bowers? Else how is it that you know how secretly, how very secretly and silently my poor heart has worshipped you all these years?"

This was the first time that the pair had looked upon one another in the plain light of day. Each, looking at the other, thought, "Who else is there like you? In all this wide world, with its oceans and rivers and all its pleasant places of habitation for the sons and daughters of men, is there anyone else so strong, so sweet, so delightful, so vividly alive and yet so restful, with laughter so easy and yet so becomingly reserved? Here is an old, old friend," they thought, "and yet how ravishingly new and strange! Newer and more wonderful at each moment, dear and familiar, yet unaccountably distant and formidable, treasured in the memory and yet never seen before,—a being such as I have never seen before, such as I shall never see again. Ah, happy day, ah, love's sweet miracle!"

It was the girl who spoke first—not without difficulty and embarrassment at first, for tears struggled with laughter in her charming voice.

"Must I remind you, sir", she said, "that so far you have only told me about your little beggar maid, and have not condescended to inform me of your business with *me*?"

Ah, Radharani! Was that the way to address the man, the sight of whom brought happy tears to your eyes, him, whom the devotion of years moved you to address in the timehonoured Hindu phrases of love and admiration, "my soul's lord," "sole possession of thy poor slave," "the sole object of longing in absence?" And yet how natural that you should rejoice in your maidenly superiority, should wish to provoke him by asking what the little beggar maid Radharani was to you! And again there rose the thought that, after all these long years, the god of your idolatry had condescended to become incarnate for your joy!

It is not for me to describe the thoughts that perplexed the maiden's bosom. Let my lady readers, learned doubtless in love's lore, imagine the situation, and think what an inexperienced maiden ought to have said under such novel and exciting circumstances. Meanwhile, let me admit that Radharani was a little astonished at her own audacity. As the words came from her lips, they had a strange sound of authority—as if she were scolding an authorised lover!

In truth Rukmini Kumar seemed a little abashed as he gently replied, "I was coming to that. At sight of you, the little maiden of long ago came into my mind. It seemed to me—vaguely—it was like the glimmer of a firefly in a dark night—a faint hope arose that this fair Radharani before me might be—*my* Radharani!"

"*Your* Radharani, sir!" cried the girl, in pretended indignation, smiling as she spoke, however, at her own disingenuousness, for indeed a smile would come to her lips, though she had to simulate maidenly scorn of rash pretensions.

But Rukmini Kumar caught the significant inflexion of her happy voice, noted joyously that she used the familiar personal pronoun instead of the formal Hindu mode of address.

"Yes," he said, "it is *my* Radharani. I only saw her once—if indeed I can rightly say I saw her at all, so dark and stormy was the night. Eight years have elapsed, and yet I know I am not mistaken. It is my Radharani!"

The girl said, in a graver tone, "Well, sir, suppose it be your Radharani, what then?"

Rukmini continued, "It was with the fainted hope that it might be my little friend of so long ago that I asked Kamakhya

Babu's eldest son, 'who is this Radharani?' For some reason or other, my friend seemed unwilling to enter into particulars. He merely said evasively, 'She is the daughter of an old friend of the family.' Seeing his reticence, I thought it improper to press him. I ventured to ask, however, why Radharani had made search for Rukmini Kumar. I told him that I thought I might be able to give some information on the subject if necessary. He replied that he himself knew nothing about the matter. His late father had regarded it as a confidential business. But his sister was in the secret, and since I knew something of the mysterious stranger he would consult his sister. With these words he departed. When he came back, he had the letter in his hand which I ventured to submit as my credentials to-day. He informed me that his sister was unable to give him any definite information, but wished me to take her letter and present it to you in person. I have carried out her instructions. Tell me, madam, if I have offended in doing so."

Radharani replied, "Sir, you have offended. Perhaps I may tell you the nature of your offence afterwards. For the present, let me say this much. Your visit to me has been prompted by a serious mistake. Who the Radharani of whom you are pleased to speak may be, I do not know. If you will tell me the story of your meeting with her, I may possibly be in a position to give you further information."

Rukmini Kumar told the whole story of the interrupted Car Festival, of the little girl's disappointment and terror, of how he had helped her home to her little wayside cottage. He omitted to give any account of his own kindness and generosity.

"I asked the question," said Radharani, "because I wanted to see if I could summon up courage to tell a stranger wherein he had offended. Forgive me, sir, if I find that I dare not tell you. If I may judge by your story, you are wanting in kindness and generosity. Consider, sir, if you were of a kindly and merciful temper, would you not have done something to relieve the necessities of a mother and daughter reduced to such cruel privations? You seem from your own account to have forgotten to come to their assistance."

"It is true," answered Rukmini Kumar, "that I was able to do little to help them. I had come by boat to witness the Car Festival. As usual I was travelling in disguise, and under my assumed name. In the afternoon a violent storm of wind and rain came on. I was afraid to remain in the doubtful shelter of a leaky boat, and preferred to face the storm on shore. What little money I had on my person—it was little enough—I gave to the girl. I intended to have returned next morning to make more particular enquiries concerning my new friends. But that very night tidings reached me that my father was grievously ill at Benares. It was a year and more before I returned from the Sacred City. When I reached home I sought out the little cottage, but mother and daughter were gone."

"May I now beg you," continued the girl, "to tell me why you seem to have so strong an affection for this little Radharani? You will excuse a woman's natural curiosity in such a matter. I gather that in the storm and tempest of which you speak, soaked with rain and buffeted with the wind, you took shelter in your young friend's cottage. May I ask how long you stayed there?"

"A few moments only," he replied. "The girl bade me wait while she kindled a light. I took the opportunity to slip away to the adjacent bazaar to buy her a change of raiment."

"Did you make her any other gift?"

"What else could I give her? Yes, I remember, I happened to have a currency note of small value about me. I left it in their cottage."

"Will you excuse me for just one moment? I shall be back presently."

Radharani had kept the note carefully all this while. She took it out of the receptacle where it was stored, and returned.

"It was foolish," she said, "to leave a currency note like that with two poor women. They would think you had lost it."

"Not so," said Rukmini Kumar, "I scribbled the words 'for Radharani' on it in pencil. I also signed my assumed name, Rukmini Kumar Ray. Otherwise my new friends might deem it a duty to make search for me, and I wished to save them the trouble."

"Ah, sir," cried Radharani, "there was the offence you have so cruelly committed. Did you not think how unkind it was not to give a grateful girl the chance of thanking her benefactor all these years? See now, whether your Radharani had cause to seek for the friend who aided her in her adversity!"

With these words she put the note in his hand, and falling in obeisance at his feet, cried, "Lord and master, that day your kindness saved my dear mother's life. In this cruel hard world, sir, it is to you that I address my devotions, and to you alone!"

VI.

When the young pair were a little recovered from the emotion of this sentimental interview, Radharani said,

"You have told me, sir, that your name is not really Rukmini Kumar. May your obedient servant know by what name she is to address her benefactor?"

"My name, madam, is Devendranath Ray."

"I have heard people speak of the Raja Devendranath Ray."

"The countryfolk give me that title. If you will call me the Kumar Devendranath Ray, I shall be sufficiently honoured."

"In that case, I am encouraged to make a daring request. Since I have now learned that we are caste-fellows, may I hope that my kind benefactor will accept my hospitality to-day?"

The raja graciously said, "Madam, since it is your wish, it would grieve me to depart without breaking bread under your roof."

By his mistress's orders the head bailiff conducted the raja to the men's apartments, and made suitable arrangements for his comfort. At the due time a collation was served to him, and his fair hostess herself waited upon her honoured guest.

When the meal was over, Radharani said, "For many years I have cherished the hope that I might have the joy of paying my respects and showing my gratitude to my benefactor. I had indeed prepared a little present which I will beg your highness to accept. This necklace is of little intrinsic value, but perhaps your highness's honoured lady will condescend to wear it as a favour to one who has reason to feel grateful to you and yours."

So saying, Radharani offered her guest a magnificent necklace, as brilliant as the glittering row of the zodiacal stars in the midnight sky.

But the raja replied, "My honoured lady, the wife of my childhood died ten years ago. I have never married again."

Radharani was filled with joy and confusion. She strove to control herself. But it was with broken and eagerly uttered words that she said, "Still, sir, I must beg you to accept the gift your servant has prepared for you. Have I your highness's gracious permission to put this poor necklace on your honoured neck?"

With these words, the girl, smiling and blushing, put the splendid and glittering ornament round the raja's neck.

Devendranath laughed to see himself thus gorgeously adorned.

"Is this beautiful necklace really mine?" he asked.

"If you be pleased to accept it."

"I accept it", he replied gravely. "And since it is now mine, may I give it to whom I will?"

"What is not worthy to be worn by your highness—such is the practice of princes—may be conferred upon any fitting person."

"This necklace is not fitted for my wearing, or rather, it is I who am not worthy to wear it. You alone are lovely enough to wear so lovely an adornment. Let me present it to you."

In such fashion, of old time, did man and maid contract marriage by an interchange of garlands. The raja clasped the necklace round Radharani's slim and graceful neck.

Radharani was not displeased. She hung down her head for a moment, and then glanced at her guest with amused and mischievous eyes. The raja understood her thoughts.

"I could, not accept that necklace, as you know, and so gave it to you. But will you give me another one?"

"Which one?"

"The one you wear, warm from your own bosom."

Radharani called to a maidservant. "Chitra!" she cried, "are you there?"

Chitra, let me observe, was watching these astonishing proceedings from behind a curtain. "Here I am, mistress," she said.

Radharani said, "Where is your conch?" (I should explain to Western readers that conch shells are blown by women on joyous and auspicious occasions.)

Chitra replied, "Mistress, here it is!"

"Well then," said Radharani joyfully, "blow your loudest!"

And then the gracious maiden with a smile loosed her own necklace, warm and fragrant from her bosom, and clasped it round her lover's neck. Chitra blew a loud blast on her conch, to warn all and sundry that a very important event had taken place!

Do you ask me whether the young pair were duly married? Of course they were married, and Vasanta came to the wedding, and all her many brothers came, and flocks of the raja's people came. But surely you have heard enough of Radharani's trials and happiness.

THE TWO RINGS

I.

A YOUTHFUL pair were standing in a leafy arbour in a garden. At that distant period the blue waters of the Bay of Bengal washed the feet of the ancient city of Tamluk, and the roar of its breakers could be heard in its streets. There stood a noble mansion in a suburb of Tamluk, and hard by on the seashore was a beautiful garden-house. These pleasant possessions belonged to a merchant of the name of Dhana Das. It was the merchant's lovely daughter Hiranmayi who was now conversing with a handsome youth in the arbour.

It must be admitted that Hiranmayi had passed the age at which Hindu girls are usually given in marriage. Not, be it observed, because of any reluctance on her part. Ever since her eleventh birthday, for five long years the girl had addressed her prayers to Sagareswari, the sea-goddess, to grant her the husband of her choice, but so far her heart's desire had not been fulfilled. Lest, however, my reader should be scandalised, let me explain that everyone knew why this marriageable maiden had, contrary to Hindu rules of propriety, granted one private interview to her young companion. When Hiranmayi was about four, the youth now by her side was eight years old. His father, Suchisuta Chetty, was a near neighbour of Dhana Das, and so the two children used to play together. They were always in one another's company in the house of one or other of their parents. Though the maiden was now sixteen years old and the boy had become a fine stripling of twenty, the old childish familiarity and friendship endured. There had been only one impediment to the continuance of these affectionate relations. At the proper season, their parents had agreed that the young people should be joined in marriage. Even the wedding day had been fixed. But, to the surprise of all, Hiranmayi's father had suddenly announced that he would not give his daughter to his old friend's son. After this decision it was of course unfitting that the girl should be on intimate terms with the friend of her childhood. It was only to-day that, by dint of repeated entreaties, and on the pretext of having a very particular communication to make her, Purandar had persuaded Hiranmayi to grant him an interview. As she entered the arbour where the youth was awaiting her, Hiranmayi hastened to say, "Why have you sent for me? You know quite well that I am no longer a little girl, and that it is improper for us to meet alone. If you send for me again, I shall not come."

It was pretty to see the grave matronly air with which this sweet sixteen year girl said, "You know I am no longer a little girl". But, alas, there was no one there to enjoy the humour of the situation. Purandar's age and mood alike prevented him from feeling the quaintness of the girl's protest.

He plucked a flower from the creeper that climbed the arbour, and began distractedly pulling it to pieces.

"I shall never ask you to come again," he said, sadly. "I am going to a far country. I wanted to tell you before I depart."

"To a far country!" She exclaimed. "Where are you going?"

"To Ceylon,[1]" he replied.

"To Ceylon!" she said. "Why is that? Why to Ceylon?"

"Why am I going?" he answered. "Because we are merchant folk, and travel by sea is our business."

As he spoke, in spite of his efforts, the lad's eyes filled with tears. Hiranmayi seemed as though she had not heard. She said not a word. Her looks wandered to the fair scene about her. Her wide-open girlish eyes seemed to be gazing at the play of the sun's rays on the twinkling waves of the sea. It was early morning. A gentle breeze was blowing. The sun shone gaily on the wavelets that ran before the breeze; the long line of breakers stretched endlessly along the shore; the foam showed on the blue water like jewels on a blue dress; the white seabirds were playing on the beach in companies. Hiranmayi seemed to be watching all these lovely things: the blue sea; the white foam on the crest of the breakers; the play of the glancing sunshine on the waves. She vaguely looked at a distant ship under sail. Her eye caught a bird far away, a dot against the pure blue of the sky. Finally her glance rested on a withered flower lying on the path. With an effort she said: "Why should *you* go? On other occasions it was your father who went on these trading expeditions."

Purandar answered: "My father is an old man now, and it is time that I should earn my living. I asked leave of my father to take his place." Hiranmayi leaned her head against one of the wooden supports of the arbour. Purandar saw that her forehead was wofully puckered, that her pretty lips were trembling, that her nostrils were quivering. Presently he saw that the girl was crying.

Purandar hastily turned aside. He too looked vaguely at the surrounding objects, at sky and shore, at the city and the sea. But it was all no use. The tears would come. They were trickling down his cheek. He angrily wiped them away, and said, "That was what I came to tell you. From the very day that your father announced that he would not consent to our marriage, I made up my mind to go to Ceylon. I hope... I hope I may never come back! If ever I can manage to forget you, I will return, but not otherwise. I cannot say any more. You would not understand me if I did. But this you must hear. If all the world and all its wealth were weighed in the balance against you, my darling, I would choose you."

Having said this, the lad stepped aside, and began pacing up and down, tearing another flower to pieces. When the hateful desire to cry was a little abated, he came back, and said: "I know quite well that you love me. But sooner or later you will be someone else's bride. So you must dismiss me from your heart. Pray that you and I may never meet again."

With these words, poor Purandar hurried away. Hiranmayi sat down and wept. Restraining her grief she said to herself: "If I were to die to-day, would Purandar need to go to Ceylon? Why should I not hang myself with one of these creepers, or fling myself into yonder sea?" And then the sensible reflection came, "If I die, what will it matter to me whether Purandar goes to Ceylon or not?"

So thinking, Hiranmayi sat and wept silently.

II.

No one knew why Dhana Das had forbidden his daughter's marriage to Purandar. He had not communicated his reasons to any of his intimates. If any one asked him, he simply answered,

"I know what I am about." The curious thing was that though numerous proposals were made for Hiranmayi's hand, he rejected them all. He simply refused to discuss the matter. His wife reproached him with allowing the proper time for marriage to slip by, but he paid no attention. He merely said, "Let our Spiritual Instructor come. When he arrives we can talk about it."

Purandar departed for Ceylon. Two years passed without any occurrence worth mentioning. But Purandar did not return, and no arrangements were made for Hiranmayi's marriage. Yet the girl, now in her eighteenth year, was as lovely and attractive as a mangoe tree in full bloom in the spring time.

Not that Hiranmayi was any longer distressed at her prolonged maidenhood. If any question of marriage arose, her thoughts flew to Purandar. Her mind dwelt on his happy smiling face, fair as a flower, and set off by the crisp curling black hair around it; she thought of the brave blue cloak with gold embroidery that hung so gallantly from his manly shoulder; she remembered the brilliant rings on his fingers. She knew that she would have to marry in obedience to her father's wishes. But that would be a death in life. And yet, whether she were pleased or not at her father's reluctance to part with her, she was certainly puzzled. It was not the custom to keep girls unmarried at her age; even if no actual ceremony was performed, it was usual to settle the preliminaries. Why was it that her father would not even listen to proposals? One day, by an accident, she secured a clue to his reasons.

In the course of trade Dhana Das had got possession of a beautiful Chinese casket. It was bigger than such caskets usually are, and his wife used to keep her jewels in it. It happened that the merchant had had several new ornaments prepared as a present for his wife, who gave her old jewels, with the casket, to her daughter. When Hiranmayi was wrapping up her new acquisitions and potting *[sic]* them away, she found half of a torn piece of paper in the casket.

Hiranmayi was well educated and could read. At the first glance at the paper, she was astonished to see her own name. She looked at the fragment, but could make no sense of what was written on it, nor could she guess the writer or recipient of the communication. Nevertheless a strange sense of fear came over her as she read the mysterious words before her. The writing was to the following effect:

> By examination of the stars I obs
> a golden image such as Hiranmayi
> age would cause terrible misfortune.
> years see one another
> they may be.

A fear of some unknown and impending misfortune filled the girl's mind. She put the scrap of paper away carefully without telling any one of her discovery.

III.

After the two years just mentioned, another year slipped by, and yet there was no talk of Purandar's return from Ceylon. But Hiranmayi's heart was still constant to his image, and the girl was sure that he too had not forgotten her. Else he would have returned.

When the third year had elapsed, Dhana Das suddenly announced that he had determined to take his family to Benares. A disciple had come from his Spiritual Instructor with orders to proceed to the ancient place of pilgrimage. Hiranmayi's marriage was at last to take place at Benares. The Spiritual Instructor had chosen a bridegroom there.

Dhana Das with his wife and daughter duly travelled to Benares. Soon after their arrival in the sacred city, Dhana Das's *guru*, Ananda Swami, paid them a visit, and, having fixed the date of the wedding, directed that all arrangements should be made in accordance with the holy Shastras. All preparations were duly performed, with one exception. There were none of the usual public announcements. Save the merchant's own family, none knew that a marriage was so soon to take place. The indispensable religious preliminaries alone were accomplished.

It was the evening of the wedding day. The auspicious junction of the stars was at nine in the evening. Up to the last moment, there was no one present except the ordinary occupants of the house. Not even any of the neighbours had been invited. So far, no one save Dhana Das himself knew who the bridegroom was, or whence he was coming. Still all were convinced that since it was Ananda Swami who had selected the bridegroom, the choice must necessarily be a wise one. If he chose not to announce the young man's name, that was his business. Who could pretend to comprehend the holy man's motives? After having made due arrangements for the officiating priest and the giving away of the bride, he was seated placidly by himself in a room apart. Dhana Das was waiting outside for the bridegroom. Hiranmayi, arrayed in her bridal costume, was seated alone in her chamber. The girl thought in her mind, "A curious wedding, truly. Yet if I may not marry Purandar, what does it matter to whom I am wedded? I shall never marry the one being whom my heart has chosen!" At this moment, Dhana Das came to summon his daughter. But before conducting her to the place where the ceremony was to be performed, he carefully tied her eyes with a cloth, so that she could not see. Hiranmayi asked, "What is this, my father?"

Dhana Das replied, "Such are the holy man's orders. Do you do as I tell you. Now recite the prescribed formulæ mentally."

The girl made no reply, and her father led her by the hand to the room prepared for the marriage.

If she had been able to see when she arrived there, she would have noticed that her future husband was also blindfolded. There was no one present save the *guru*, the officiating priest, and the girl's father. Bride and bridegroom being both blind-folded, the ceremony of causing them to take the first auspicious look at one another after marriage was perforce omitted.

After the completion of the ceremony, the *guru-deva* addressed the young couple. "You are now wedded to another, but have not seen one another. The sole object of this ceremony has been to relieve the bride of the reproach of prolonged and unseasonable maidenhood. Whether you will ever see one another in this life I cannot say. If it should happen that you meet, you would not be able to recognise one another as husband and wife. For this reason, I am about to provide you with a means of recognising one another hereafter. In my hand are two rings. The stones with which they are set are extremely rare and hard to obtain. Moreover on the inner surface of each ring a peacock is engraved. I give one ring to the bride and the other to the bridegroom. No one else possesses such rings, and, further, the device inscribed in them cannot be imitated, since I have engraved it with my own hand. If the bride should ever see such a ring on a man's finger, she will know that that man is her husband. If the bridegroom should find such a ring on a woman's hand, he will recognise his affianced wife. Take care lest either of you lose the ring I give you. Do not part with it to anyone; do not sell it even if you are reduced to starvation. Furthermore, it is my order that neither of you shall wear the ring I now give you for five years from this day. Today is the fifth day of the waxing moon of the month Asharh, and the eleventh hour. It is forbidden to you to wear your rings till the corresponding date and hour of the fifth year from to-day. If you disobey this solemn injunction, terrible misfortunes will befall you."

After this admonition, Ananda Swami took his leave. Dhana Das removed the cloth from his daughter's eyes. Looking round her, Hiranmayi saw that there was no one in the room except her father and the officiating priest. Her husband had disappeared. She spent her wedding night alone.

IV.

After the wedding, Dhana Das returned home with his wife and daughter. Four more years elapsed. Purandar was still absent. After all, what did it matter to Hiranmayi now, if he did return?

Hiranmayi felt vaguely depressed at the thought that the friend of her childhood had absented himself all these seven years. "How can I believe," she thought, "that he has stayed away for so many years simply because he cannot forget me? Who knows whether he is alive or dead? It is not permitted to me to wish for the sight of him, now that I am another's wife. But why should I not hope and pray that my childhood's companion is still alive?"

About this time, her old father began to wear an anxious and harassed countenance, and finally fell seriously ill of a disease which caused his death. His wife refused to survive him. Hiranmayi had no other relatives than her parents, and entreated her mother with tears to change her fatal resolution, but the merchant's widow was obdurate. And so Hiranmayi was left all alone in the world.

Before dying, Hiranmayi's mother had tried to reassure her daughter. "See, my child," she had said, "you have no cause for anxiety. After all, you are a married woman. When the appointed interval has elapsed, who knows but you may meet your husband. You are no longer a mere girl. Above all, you have the best helper in the world, plenty of money. Your father has made due arrangements for that."

Alas, on this point the good lady was mistaken. When enquiries were made after Dhana Das's death, it was found that all his hard-won savings had disappeared. His daughter's sole possessions turned out to be her jewels, the family house, and the furniture. It seemed that for years the old man had been incurring losses in business. He had told no one of his bad investments and had struggled silently to repair his losses. Finally he had given up all hope of ever recovering his former competence. It was anxiety and business worries that had caused his illness and death.

When the news of the unfortunate merchant's failure in business spread about, creditors came and pressed Hiranmayi to pay her father's debts. She made enquiries and learned that the claims thus set up were just, and, a true merchant's daughter, sold all she had to clear her father's fair fame and pay his debts.

Reduced finally to dire need, the poor girl hired a small thatched hut on the outskirts of the town and dwelt there in extreme obscurity and poverty. Her only hope now lay in her spiritual guide, the *guru*, Ananda Swami. Unfortunately, he was then absent in a far country, nor had Hiranmayi anyone whom she could send to communicate her misfortunes to her only surviving friend and guardian.

V.

Hiranmayi was a beautiful young woman. It was not fitting that she should sleep alone in a house by herself. Not only was there obvious risk, but there might be occasion for scandalous gossip. It happened that one Amala, daughter of a milkman by caste, dwelt hard by. This woman was a widow with a baby son and some young daughters. This person had passed the age of youth and attractiveness, and had the reputation of being a woman of excellent character. So Hiranmayi used to go and spend the night in her house.

One evening, when Hiranmayi had arrived at her new friend's house, Amala said to her, "I have heard a piece of news. They say Purandar Chetty has returned home after an absence of eight years." On hearing these unexpected tidings, Hiranmayi turned away her face, lest Amala should see the sudden tears that came to her eyes. It seemed to her as if her last tie with the world was loosed. Purandar had succeeded in dismissing her from his mind. Else why should he return? On the other hand, what mattered it to her now, whether Purandar remembered or forgot her? True. Yet it went hard with her to think that he whose affection had been the guiding star of her whole life should have forgotten her. Then the thought came, "Perhaps he has not forgotten me after all! How long was he to stay away from his home? Besides his father was now dead. His presence at home was absolutely necessary." Again she thought, "I am nothing else but a wanton. Else why, being a married woman, do I think about Purandar at all?"

Amala asked, "Do you mean to say you have forgotten young Purandar? I mean Purandar, the son of Suchisuta Chetty."

Hiranmayi replied, "I remember him."

"Well, then," continued Amala, "he has come back, with ships full of treasure that cannot be counted. They say he has brought back more riches than have ever been seen in Tamluk before."

A strange pang of something like envy came into Hiranmayi's heart. She remembered her own poverty, and the old arrangement that she was to be Purandar's wife. The pain of poverty is a thing grievous to be borne, and all these riches of which Amala spoke might have been hers. There are few women who would not have felt the contrast between her actual state and what might have been. For a while Hiranmayi remained wrapped in thought. Then she turned the conversation to other matters. Finally, as the women were retiring to rest, she suddenly asked, "Amala, has the young merchant a wife?"

Amala replied, "No, he is not married."

A strange commotion came over Hiranmayi's spirits. For a moment she thought—but no, she would ask no more questions. She retired silently to rest.

VI.

Some time after, Amala came to Hiranmayi with a good-natured grin on her homely face and said, "Well, young woman, what am I to think of your manners and morals now?"

Hiranmayi asked, "What have I been doing now?"

"Why did you not tell me all this time?"

"What was there to tell?"

"That you were such a dear friend of Purandar Chetty, to be sure!"

Hiranmayi's face flushed with shame at this sudden imputation. She said, however, "Well, they were neighbours of ours when I was a child. There was nothing else to tell."

"Merely neighbours? Look here, what I have brought!"

So saying, Amala produced a casket. Opening it, she displayed a real marvel, a diamond necklace of extreme beauty and enormous value. The merchant's daughter was a judge of precious stones. She said in astonishment, "But this is worth a prince's ransom! Where did you get this?"

"Purandar has sent it to you. Hearing that you were lodging in my house, he sent for me and bade me give you this from him."

Hiranmayi reflected a moment. She knew that if she accepted so princely a gift, she would be relieved of all fear of want. The only daughter of a wealthy merchant, accustomed to luxury all her life, she was beginning to feel the pangs of poverty very cruelly. For a moment, she hesitated. But finally she sighed and said, "Amala, take this back to the merchant, and say I cannot accept it."

Amala was surprised. "What is this?" she cried. "Have you lost your senses, or don't you believe what I am telling you?"

"My dear," replied Hiranmayi gently, "I believe every word you say, and I am in full possession of my senses. But I cannot accept such a gift."

Amala argued with her in vain. Hiranmayi utterly refused to be persuaded. Finally Amala took the necklace to the raja of the place, known by the name of Raja Madan Deva. Making her prostration before this nobleman, she said to him, "Your honour will be pleased to accept this jewel. You alone are worthy to possess so costly a thing." The raja accepted the necklace, and gave a suitably magnificent reward to Amala. Of course Hiranmayi was not told of this transaction.

A few days after this, one of Purandar's maidservants came to Hiranmayi and said, "My master has sent me to tell you that he cannot bear the thought of your living in this thatched hut. You are the companion of his boyhood. Your father's house is as a second home to him. Of course he does not venture to suggest that you should take up your abode in his house. But he has bought your father's old home from his creditors, and wishes to make you a present of it. He begs as a favour to him to accept your old home from him as a gift."

Of all the consequences of poverty, the most painful to Hiranmayi's mind was her banishment from the home of her childhood. The thought was cruel that she might not end her days in the dear home where she had played as a child, where her father and mother had spent so many happy years, where she had seen them die. The mere mention of the old home brought tears to her eyes.

She thanked and blessed the servant girl and said, "I know I ought not to accept this gift. But I cannot restrain the desire that possesses me. May all happiness and good fortune attend your master!"

The girl made her obeisance and departed. Amala was present during this interview. Hiranmayi said to her, "It will be impossible for me to dwell there alone. You must come and live with me."

Amala agreed to this, and removed to Dhana Das's old home with her young mistress.

Nevertheless Hiranmayi forbad Amala to pay any more visits to Purandar's house, and, let us hope, was obeyed.

On one point Hiranmayi was much puzzled, after taking up her abode in her old home. One day Amala said to her, "There is no need for you to worry about money matters any more, or to perform any bodily labour. I have got work in the raja's palace, and shall not want for money any more. I will take charge of the house-keeping, but, of course, I shall always regard you as my mistress."

As a matter of fact, she noticed Amala seemed to have plenty of money to spend, and began to entertain the most uncomfortable suspicions.

VII.

And now at last the fifth day of the waxing moon of the month Asharh of the fifth year after Hiranmayi's marriage had come round. Remembering this fact, she was seated absorbed in thought as the dusk of evening drew on. She was thinking, "By the *guru's* order I can wear my ring to-morrow. But shall I put it on? What is the good? I may perhaps find my husband by means of it. But do I want to find him? Why is another's image always imprinted in my heart? My plain duty is to control and punish my wicked heart. Otherwise I shall fall into deadly sin."

At this moment Amala arrived in a state of high excitement and astonishment.

"Here is a fine business," she cried, "I don't know what to make of it! What will happen next?"

"What is the matter?" asked Hiranmayi.

"Why a whole crowd of menservants and maidservants have come with a palanquin with orders to convey you to the raja's palace."

"You have lost your senses, foolish woman. Why on earth should they want to take me to the raja's palace?"

True enough, however, one of the raja's maids here made her appearance and, making due obesiance *[sic]*, said, "It is the order of my master, may the holy gods prolong his days, that Hiranmayi shall at once accompany us to his palace."

Hiranmayi was amazed, but did not dare to refuse. The raja's orders could not be disobeyed. Moreover there was no occasion for fearing to enter Raja Madan Deva's palace. The Raja enjoyed the highest reputation for kindness and virtue. Not only was he virtuous himself, but owing to his vigilance no woman ran any risk of insult or annoyance under his roof.

Hiranmayi said to Amala, "I agree to pay my respects to the raja. Come you with me."

Amala agreed to go, and her mistress, mounting into the palanquin, was carried to the palace in great state. A maidservant conveyed the news of Hiranmayi's arrival to the raja and presently returned to escort our heroine to the presence.

Amala remained outside, in much impatience and curiosity.

VIII.

Hiranmayi was much impressed by the raja's aspect. He was a tall handsome man of noble presence, broad-chested and of martial looks; his forehead was lofty, his eyes large and piercing, his demeanour dignified. Not often does a zenana woman see so imposing and attractive a male being. The raja too recognised that even in royal palaces maidens so lovely as the merchant's daughter are not often encountered.

The raja asked, "Is this Hiranmayi?"

Hiranmayi replied, "I am your highness's humble servant."

The raja said, "Hear now why I have sent for you. Do you remember the night of your wedding?"

Hiranmayi replied, "Indeed, sir, I do remember."

"Have you still got the ring which Ananda Swami gave you that night?"

"Maharaj, I have it still. But these are very secret matters. How has your highness cognisance of them?"

Instead of answering this question, the raja said, "Where is your ring? Show it to me."

Hiranmayi replied, "I have left it at home. An hour or more is still wanting till the five years are completed. Therefore I must still obey the Swami's orders forbidding me to wear the ring."

"Well and good. But do you think you could recognise the corresponding ring which Ananda Swami gave to your husband to keep?"

"Both rings were exactly alike. I should of course recognise the other ring from its likeness to mine."

At this, on a sign from the raja, the attendant maid-servant fetched a small casket. The raja, taking a ring from this casket, handed it to Hiranmayi, and said,

"Look at this. Is this the ring?"

Hiranmayi carefully examined it by the light of a lamp, and said,

"Deva, this is in truth my husband's ring. But where did your highness procure it?"

After reflecting a moment, she added,

"Deva, by the sight of this I know that I am a widow. This must have come into your highness's hands by the death of my husband, since such windfalls are your highness's prerogrative *[sic]* as the ruler of this place. Otherwise my husband would certainly never have dared to part with it."

The raja laughed and said, "Take my word for it, madam, you are no widow."

"Then, in that case my husband is even poorer than myself. He must have sold it under pressure of dire want."

"On the contrary, your husband is a wealthy man."

"Then you must have taken the ring from my husband by force or fraud."

The raja was a little astonished at this daring speech. He said, "You are a very rash young woman! No one ever yet charged Raja Madan Deva with being a robber or a cheat!"

"Well, but how did the ring come into your highness's hands?"

"Ananda Swami put it on my finger on the night of your wedding!"

Hiranmayi hung her head with shame at this announcement. She said, "My prince, forgive your handmaiden's offence. I am but a witless being, and have sinned from ignorance."

IX.

Hiranmayi was much astonished at hearing that she was the wife of so exalted a personage. But she experienced neither pride nor pleasure. Rather was she depressed in spirits. She reflected, "All this time I have been separated from Purandar, it is true, but at least I have not been married to any one else. From this time forth I must know the pain of loveless marriage. Besides I am Purandar's wife in my heart. How shall I, loving another, desecrate this great man's home by being his wife?"

Her mind was busy with such thoughts when the Raja said:

"Hiranmayi, you are my spouse indeed. But before taking you to myself, there are some questions I must beg you to answer. How is it that you are living in Purandar's house without paying any rent?"

Hiranmayi stood abashed with downcast looks.

Again the raja asked, "Why is your servant Amala always going to and from Purandar's residence?"

Hiranmayi was still more abashed and distressed. She thought to herself, "Is the raja omniscient?"

The raja went on, "There is another very important matter. Why did you, a married woman, accept a necklace of enormous value from Purandar?"

This time Hiranmayi summoned up courage to reply,

"My prince, I find that you are not omniscient. I returned that necklace."

"Not so, you sold it to me. Look, here it is."

So saying, the raja took the necklace from the casket and showed it to her. She recognised it at once, and was completely non-plussed. She said, however,

"My prince, did I myself bring this necklace to you for sale?"

"No, but your servant or messenger Amala brought it to me. Shall I send for her?"

Hiranmayi was vexed, but could not refrain from smiling at a happy thought that now occurred to her. Hastily she answered,

"My prince, I admit my guilt. There is no need to send for Amala. I admit that I sold you the necklace!"

This time it was the raja's turn to be astonished. He said,

"Woman's ways are past comprehension. How did you, a married woman, come to accept such a gift from Purandar?"

"I accepted it as a token of his passionate love for me!"

The raja was still more astonished.

"What do you mean?" he asked. "What sort of love do you mean?"

"My prince," she cried, "I am a wicked woman. I am not worthy to be your wife. I make my obeisance. Suffer me to depart. Forget that you were ever wedded to me."

Hiranmayi bowed low and was about to depart when the raja's puzzled face was irradiated by a jovial smile. He laughed aloud.

Hiranmayi turned her face towards him.

"Hiranmayi!" he cried, "you have beaten me fairly! I have lost the battle of wits. Look, you are not a wicked woman, nor am I your husband! Do not go yet."

"Maharaj," she replied, "will you then explain to your servant what all this business means? I am only a poor woman. Can I believe that so exalted a personage is pleased to amuse himself at your servant's expense?"

The raja, still laughing, said, "My good lady, great people like me are fond of such mystifications. Now tell me. Six years ago, did you not find half of a torn scrap of paper among your jewels? Have you got it still?"

"Maharaj, your highness is omniscient, after all! I have got the paper by me still."

"Well, then," said the raja, "get into the palanquin again, go home, and fetch me the paper. When you have brought it to me I will tell you everything."

X.

Hiranmayi, in obedience to the raja's commands, entered her palanquin, returned home, and having procured the torn scrap of paper of which we have already spoken, conveyed it to the raja, who, after carefully examining it, produced a similar fragment and gave it to Hiranmayi. He told her to put the two pieces of paper together. On doing so, she found that the two edges fitted one another.

"Read, now, what is written," said the raja.

Hiranmayi read as follows:—

"(By examination of the stars I observed) that the plans you have made are inauspicious. (A golden image such as Hiranmayi) should not be submitted to the risk of long widowhood. Her marriage would cause terrible misfortune. I have found by astrological calculation that she will be a widow at an early age. Nevertheless, if husband and wife do not for five years (see one another), in that case I may be able to indicate a line of action whereby (they may be) able to escape from the evil planetary influences which threaten them."

When Hiranmayi had read this, the raja said,

"This paper was given to your father by Ananda Swami."

"So I now understand," said Hiranmayi. "I see now why our eyes were blindfolded at our wedding, why the ceremony was performed in so extraordinary and secret a fashion, why we were forbidden to wear our rings during five years. This much I understand, but the rest is still a mystery to me."

"Surely you comprehend," replied the raja, "why your father on receiving this communication suspended the negotiation for your marriage with Purandar, and why Purandar himself in despair undertook the voyage to Ceylon. Meanwhile Ananda Swami was making enquiries for a suitable and auspicious bridegroom. His search was successful. On examining the young man's horoscope, he found that he was destined to reach the age of eighty years, if he should escape a risk of death at the age of twenty-eight. By his learned calculations he ascertained that before the youth had attained to that age, and within five years of his marriage, he would incur a terrible risk of dying in his nuptial couch. But the stars showed plainly that if he could survive these fateful five years, he would live to a good old age.

"It was therefore settled that the marriage should take place when the bridegroom was twenty-three years old. But there was also the fear that if you remain seemingly unmarried all these years you might commit some imprudent act, or secretly marry someone else. That was why, in order to frighten you, the torn scrap of paper was left in your jewel casket. You know already how arrangements were made that you should not have sight of your husband during the five years of probation. It was precisely for that reason that you were prevented from seeing one another during the ceremony.

"But, a few months ago, all these wise and careful provisions were much disturbed by the unexpected course of events. When Ananda Swami came here secretly a few months ago he was much grieved to learn that you had been reduced to poverty. He got a glimpse of you, though you were not aware of the fact. He came to me however, and informed me of all the romantic incidents of your marriage. He told me that if he could have guessed what hardships were destined to befall you, he would have made arrangements for a suitable maintenance for you. He entrusted the task of providing for your comfort to me, and made himself responsible for any expenditure I might incur. Moreover he laid this injunction upon me. Your husband, so he informed me, is an inhabitant of this city and he desired me to take such measures as would make it impossible for you and him to meet. He has told me who your husband is. Since that time I have supplied Amala with the funds required to keep you in health and comfort. It was really I who purchased your father's house and caused you to enter into occupation of it. It was I who sent you the diamond necklace. That was to test your fidielity *[sic]*."

"Where, then," asked Hiranmayi, "did your highness procure this ring? Why did you put me to pain and shame by pretending that you yourself were my lord and master? Why, too, did you allow me to remain in the belief that I was Purandar's tenant and under obligations to him?"

"From the day that I received Ananda Swami's orders", replied the raja, "I appointed people to watch over you. Then it was that I instructed Amala to tempt you with the offer of the necklace. Finally, knowing that to-day your long probation is concluded, I sent for your husband and told him that I was acquainted with all the strange circumstances of your lives, I told him that to-day his wife would at last be entrusted to him. 'With all due submission to your highness's orders,' he said, 'I have no desire whatever to see her. Better far that we should not meet.' I replied, nevertheless, 'Such are my orders.' He of course agreed that he had no course but to obey. 'But,' he objected, 'it is your highness only who knows what her life has been during these years and whether she is fitted to take her place in an honest gentleman's home. I take it that a personage of your highness's rank and reputation would not ask me to live with a woman who has been the object of scandal.' In reply I bade him leave his ring with me, telling him that by its means I would make test of your fidelity to your marriage vows. He paid me the compliment of saying that he would not have entrusted the ring to anyone else in the world, but that in my case he had no scruples. Let me hasten to add that you have triumphantly sustained the little test to which I subjected you."

"But," objected Hiranmayi, "I do not even now understand the nature of the test to which your highness was pleased to subject his humble servant!"

Even as she spoke, the lofty halls of the palace resounded with joyous nuptial music. "The eleventh hour has struck," said the raja, "I will tell you about the test of your now proved constancy later. Your husband has arrived. Your first sight of him occurs at an auspicious moment."

At this moment a door behind Hiranmayi was thrown open. A tall and handsome man stepped gravely into the chamber. The raja said,

"Hiranmayi, let me present you to your husband!"

Hiranmayi looked up; her brain reeled; she knew not whether she was awake or dreaming. For the newcomer was—Purandar!

The happy pair stood, too astonished to move or speak, neither could believe the joy that had befallen them.

The raja said, "Friend, Hiranmayi deserves all your love and respect. Take her, sir, with all due affection to your home. To this day she loves you as dearly as she has always loved you. Day and night I have had her under careful observation, and I know that her heart is wholly yours. At your request, sir, I subjected her to a wholly unnecessary trial. I went so far as to inform her that she was in fact my own wife. Not even the thought of princely honours shook her heartwhole devotion to you. I hinted to her that, though she was my wedded wife, I suspected her of a guilty passion for you. If she had been offended at a charge so revolting to her womanly modesty, if she had asserted her innocence, and had begged me to take her to my arms, I should have known that she had forgotten her lifelong affection for you. What do you think, sir, was this gentle creature's answer to a most offensive accusation? 'I am a guilty woman,' she said, 'and not worthy to be your highness's wife.' Hiranmayi, it was with pleasure and respect that I comprehended the motive that led a good woman to accept a cruel and false insinuation. Rather than yield yourself to a union without love, you were willing to endure a slanderous accusation. My child, with all my heart, I wish you and your husband all happiness!"

But even now Hiranmayi was not fully satisfied.

"Maharaj," she said, "satisfy your servant's curiosity on one other point. If Purandar was absent in Ceylon, how was it that he was able to be present at the wedding in Benares? And if he was able to proceed to the Sacred City at that time, how was it that we were all kept in ignorance of the fact?"

"Ah," said the raja, "that is easily explained. The Swami and Purandar's father arranged that your husband should go straight to Benares from Ceylon and return thither when the marriage ceremony was completed. He did not visit his home on the way. That is how his movements were concealed from the gossips of my excellent town of Tamluk."

Purandar here bowed low and said, "Maharaj, as your highness has to-day fulfilled my heart's dearest desire, so may kind Providence fulfil your highness's every wish. In all your highness's dominions there is no happier man to-day than your highness's humble slave and subject, Purandar Chetty."

---

1. Of course Ceylon in the old days of sailing ships was as the Antipodes in our own time.

DOCTOR MACRURUS

OR

Vyaghracharya Brihallangul[1]

I.

Once upon a time, the tiger folk held a great Congress in the forests of the Sunderbans. On a plot of rising ground in the heart of the woods sat row upon row of the great beasts, the gleam of their shining teeth showing bravely in the dense gloom of the jungle. By an unanimous vote, an aged tiger named Gastrimargos[2] had been chosen to preside over their deliberations. The honourable Gastrimargos, sitting up gravely, and supported by his tail, began the business of the meeting by thus addressing the distinguished assemblage.

"This is a memorable day in the annals of our race. I see before me, gathered together to discuss matters relating to our common welfare, the most eminent members of our ancient, famous, sylvan and carnivorous community. Alas, other animals, envious and slanderous creatures, have spread the report that we are unsocial, divided, inhabiting each his own patch of jungle, incapable of united action. One of the principal objects of this unexampled gathering is to refute this unfounded and wicked aspersion. So rapidly are we advancing in civilisation, that we may well cherish the hope that we shall soon be counted among the most cultivated and polished of living beings. It is my highest aspiration that, by means of such concerted action as we have now adopted, we may be able to pursue our ancestral trade of preying upon other animals in peace and prosperity." (Loud applause by slapping of tails on the ground.) "And now, my brethren, let me briefly announce the particular business for which you have been convened. You are all only too well aware that of late years there has been a lamentable falling off of polite instruction among us. The fact is indisputable; the remedy is easy. There has arisen a very real desire for education among us. Nowadays, it may be said, all sorts and conditions of animals are educated. Why should we not follow this example? This Congress has gathered to discuss the educational needs of our race. With these few words, I declare the meeting open, and invite you to begin your discussion of the important matters which will be submitted to you."

The assemblage indicated their approval of this brief oration by vigorous growls and roarings. Various resolutions were then read and supported by extremely long speeches, which, inspite of the correctness of the grammar and the excellence of the rhetoric employed in them, were, it must be admitted, terrific in utterance. In truth the woods trembled at the sound of oratory so sonorous. When other business had been transacted, the president sat up and said, "You are all no doubt aware that a *savant* among tigers, the illustrious Megalopygos,[3] inhabits these forests. This learned gentleman has kindly consented to read a paper to us to-night, taking as his subject, "The Natural History of Man"."

At mention of the word 'man', several of the younger tigers present felt a sensation of hunger, but seeing no preparations for a public banquet, put a tactful restraint on their instinctive desire to express their sentiments. The learned lecturer, at the president's invitation, arose with a courteous growl and, in a voice calculated to fill the wayfarer with terror, delivered the following discourse:—

"Mr. President, Ladies and Gentlemen,

Men, from one point of view, may be regarded as bipeds. They are, however, unprovided with feathers, and cannot therefore be called birds. On the other hand, they have many points in common with quadrupeds. Their limbs and osteology resemble those of quadrupeds. On a general consideration of their physical structure, they may, I think, fairly be included among the four-footed animals. It is true that they lack the comeliness and force of other quadrupeds, but it would not be fair, merely on this account, to classify them among birds and other mere bipeds.

Among fourfooted beasts, they bear the closest resemblance to monkeys. Men of science tell us that it is possible, in the course of many generations, for animals to develop missing limbs and wanting faculties, and so to rise in the scale of creation. It is permitted to us to entertain the hope that men may, in their progressive evolution, develop tails and rise to the dignity of being monkeys.

"You are all, no doubt, aware that men are agreeable to the taste and furnish digestible and nourishing food." (At these words the members of the audience licked their lips.) "You also know that they fall an easy prey to our noble race. Unlike deer, they are not swift of flight; unlike the buffaloes of our native woods, they have neither horns nor the strength to use them. No reasonable person can doubt that they were created by bountiful Providence solely for the use of tigers, and hence were unprovided with means of escape or defence. But for this obvious consideration it would be difficult to imagine what possible purpose could be served by the existence of a species so feeble and so ill prepared for the competitive struggle of life. Let us, without further argument, admit that they are good for food. For many reasons, and especially on account of the tenderness of their flesh, we are all very fond of men. What may surprise you is the undoubted fact that these creatures are equally fond of us! If any gentleman present is inclined to throw doubt on this assertion, let me, by way of proof, state my own humble experience in the matter. I may perhaps without arrogance claim that in the course of my investigations I have travelled more widely than anyone here to-night. During my wanderings, I happened to journey to the north of these famous Sunderbans, the chosen home of our illustrious race. I found myself in a land inhabited by cows, men and other defenceless and harmless creatures. The men there are of two species, black and white in colour. I happened to be out one day on business."

An inquisitive tiger of the name of Odontokeros[4] ventured to interrupt with the question, "May I ask what the learned lecturer means by the word 'business'?"

"Business", replied the lecturer, "is, briefly, the search for food. Civilised races nowadays invariably use this euphemism. I must, however, admit that this universal occupation cannot always be justly described by this term. In the case of exalted and respectable persons it may rightly be called 'business'; when inferior people hunt for provendor, their task becomes thieving, domestic service, or begging. The business of dishonest persons is commonly called 'theft'; those who steal forcibly are 'robbers'. But the word 'robber' must not be used indiscriminately. Sometimes the word 'hero' must be substituted. It is only the punishable forms of exaction that are called 'robbery'. All other varieties of this pursuit are called 'heroism'. I must beg you, when mixing in polished society, to bear these distinctions in mind. Otherwise you will run the risk of being considered uncivilised. For my own part, I have come to the private conclusion that these are unnecessary refinements and that all these categories might very well be included under the one word 'gastrophily'.[5]

Be that as it may, I continue my narration, and repeat that men are extremely devoted to tigers. As I have said before, I one day wandered among the habitations of men on business. You have no doubt heard that some years ago there was established in the Sunderbans a Port Canning Company."[6]

Odontokeros again interrupted to ask what manner of beast a Port Canning Company might be.

"I cannot honestly say", admitted the lecturer, "that I am well informed on that point. I have never been able to ascertain what its external aspect was, or to what genus of living creatures it belonged. But I have been informed that it was created by men, that its drink was the heart's blood of men, and that it waxed very fat on this nourishment. I ought to mention that the race of men is extraordinarily improvident. They are perpetually occupied in devising means for their own destruction. The weapons that they use are a proof of this fact. I have heard that they will collect by thousands in an open place and deliberately slay one another with these weapons. My own belief is that this Port Canning Company was a demoniac form created by men for their mutual destruction.

That, however, is irrelevant to the subject of my discourse, and I must beg you to refrain from further interruptions. The time at my disposal is limited, and I have much that is interesting to say. Our president will support me in the statement that such interruptions are considered as breaches of order in civilised assemblies.

Once more, ladies and gentlemen, I assert that I went to Matla, the abode of this Port Canning Company, on business. I happened to see a plump and lively kid in a curious construction of stout bamboos. The entrance was open, and I entered to taste the food thus temptingly offered to me. The building was, I found, a magical one, for the door closed of itself behind me. Presently several men made their appearance. It was evident that they were overjoyed at my advent among them. They gave vent to shouts, laughter, and various uncouth exclamations of pleasure. I was able to understand that they indulged in praises of my strength and beauty. They were lost in admiration of my teeth, my claws, and, above all, my tail. Some actually affectionately addressed me by the endearing term of 'brother-in-law'[7].

Finally they respectfully raised me together with the temporary residence in which I found myself (their own name for it is a 'trap') and placed me in a cart drawn by two snow-white bullocks. I must admit that the sight of these animals filled me with the pangs of hunger, but seeing no immediate means of escaping from the magic 'trap', I took a light meal off the kid so considerately provided by my kind captors. Travelling thus in state, and feasting comfortably as I went, I was conveyed to the abode of a white man in the city. He most respectfully came to his door to give me fitting greeting, and was good enough to indicate a dwelling for me adorned with elegant iron bars. In this place he daily gratified me with offerings of living or newly slain goats and sheep. Other men of various races and conditions came to pay their respects to me and evidently acquired merit by this pious observance. I dwelt a long time in this commodious and safe place of residence. Surrounded by so many comforts and conveniences, for a while I was contented and even happy. But, before long, I began to feel the ache of homesickness. When the vision of this my sacred native land came to my memory, I gave vent to my emotion in the most pathetic roarings and howls. Ah, Motherland of the Sunderbans, could I ever forget thee? At the thought of thy dear forests, I would refuse the flesh of sheep and of goats. Or rather, to be quite accurate, I rejected their skin and bones, and revealed my disquietude to the anxious spectators by the furious lashings of my tail. Ah, land of my birth! So long as I was absent from thee, I never ate—save when I was very hungry; never slept unless I was *really sleepy*! What better proof of my grief can I give than the solemn assertion that never, no, never, did I eat more than a mere bellyful—or at most a pound or two more. Never more!"

The lecturer was so overcome by these memories that he kept silence for some time. It has been asserted that he wept, and indeed one or two drops were noticed to fall on the dry dust before him. It is possible, however, that these were due to the fact that his mouth watered at the thought of the daily meals provided during his distant exile. Recovering himself, however, he continued:—

"I need not explain at length how I came to quit this agreeable lodging. One day my attendant, after cleaning my apartment, left the door open; whether because he had guessed the pangs of homesickness from which I was suffering, or from carelessness, I shall now never know. Anyhow, I seized the opportunity—and a disappointingly lean gardener who happened to be passing—and returned to our beloved native land.

If any excuse be required for this detailed account of my adventures among the haunts of men, let me explain that my sole object is to indicate that I had abundant opportunities for making a careful and detailed study of the peculiarities of the genus men. I will tell you nothing that is not the outcome of personal observation. I am not in the habit of indulging in the shameless inventions of which some travellers have been convicted. Let me tell you, once for all, that I utterly disbelieve many tales that are current among us as to the habits and customs of men. For instance, we have been brought up in the belief that men, feeble creatures though they be, are capable of constructing lofty and substantial dwellings for themselves. All I can say is that I have never seen them in the act of erecting such buildings. There is no proof whatever that they have the power of preparing such dens for themselves. I believe for my own part that their dwellings are in fact hills, the work of nature, and that, seeing these hills to be full of caves, the more intelligent among them took up their abode in these convenient shelters.

The race of Men is what is called amphivorous, that is, they eat meat, and also fruits and roots. They cannot eat large trees, but they consume small plants, roots and all. They are so fond of small plants that they grow them in enclosed places, which they call 'fields' or 'gardens'. One man is not allowed to graze in another man's enclosure.

That they eat fruits, roots, creepers, shrubs, is now an established fact, but I am not able to assert with any certainty that they eat grass. I have never seen any man eat grass. But on this subject I have some doubt. White men and the richer black men carefully prepare plots of grass known as 'lawns.' It is probable that the grass in them is intended for food. Indeed I once overheard a black man say, "The country is going to the dogs;—all Sahebs and other big men are idly eating grass."[8] It may therefore be assumed with some approach to certainty that the upper classes of men do eat grass.

When men lose their temper, they ask, 'Do you think I eat grass!'[9] Now it is one of the peculiarities of the whole tribe to conceal the profession by which they earn their living. It is permissible to infer that those who are indignant at a suspicion of eating grass are in fact graminivorous.

Men worship animals. I have already told you of the extraordinary devotion of which I was the unworthy object. They also worship horses. They provide them with dwellings, give them food daily, and attend carefully to their toilettes. No doubt such observances are an ingenuous recognition of the superiority of horses.

On the other hand, men feed goats, sheep and cattle. I have myself observed one extraordinary fact with reference to their behaviour to cows. They drink their milk! Our older scientists accepted this as a proof that they must once have been calves. I would not go so far as this, but the fact that they consume cow's milk may perhaps account for the bovine character of their intellects. Be that as it may, men feed and keep goats, sheep and cattle for greater convenience in procuring flesh food. This is an excellent device. I look forward to the time when we shall see the convenience of erecting mensheds, and keeping and breeding these useful animals for food.

I have already told you of their care for cattle, horses, sheep and goats. But they also keep and feed elephants, camels, asses, dogs, cats, and even birds. It may therefore be said with truth that men are the natural slaves and servants of all other living creatures.

I noticed many monkeys among the abodes of men. These monkeys are of two sorts: those with tails and those without tails. The former dwell for the most part on roofs or in trees. I have seen many on the ground, it is true; but most of them occupy the more exalted position. This is probably due to some mistaken notion of racial pride.

The morals of men are extremely amusing. But their political arrangements are also very surprising. I will describe them in detail."

The lecturer had reached this point, when the respected president happened to see a fawn in the distance, and leaving the chair with a bound, started in pursuit. (I ought to explain that he had been chosen to preside precisely on account of his sharpness of vision.) The lecturer was somewhat annoyed at this proof of the president's want of interest in his exposition. Observing this, one of the most intelligent of the audience remarked:—

"Pray, sir, do not be offended by the sudden departure of our respected president. He has left us on pressing 'business'. A herd of deer approaches. *I can smell them*!"

On hearing these words, the audience, with tails high in air, rapidly dispersed 'on business', and the learned lecturer followed their example. Thus was it that the Congress came to an untimely end, for that day. When they next met, it was after taking the precaution of partaking of a copious meal. On that occasion, the remainder of the lecture was delivered without impediment. But perhaps a full and accurate report of the subsequent proceedings had better be reserved for another chapter.

II.

The lecturer resumed his discourse as follows:—

"Mr. President, Tigresses and Tigers,

I promised on a previous occasion that I would tell you something about the extraordinary marriage and other customs of men. My first and obvious duty is to fulfil that promise. I enter upon my subject at once without any preliminary apologies.

You all know what is meant by marriage. You have all from time to time contracted marriages, as occasion served. But marriage as understood by men is somewhat different. Marriage, with tigers and other civilised animals, is merely, if I may be permitted the expression, a temporary arrangement *ad hoc* between male and female on equal terms. Among men marriage is not infrequently a life-long union!

The marriage of men is of two kinds, 'regular and irregular.' Of these two kinds, the 'regular' or 'sacerdotal' form is held in the highest honour. The variety in which a priest intervenes is called a 'sacerdotal' marriage.

Mr. Odontokeros:—"May I ask the learned lecturer what a 'priest' is?"

"The dictionary definition is, 'a species of mankind that lives on rice and bananas and practises cheating.' But this description is plainly defective. For it is not true that all priests are vegetarians. Many eat flesh and drink intoxicating liquor: some are even omnivorous. Nor, on the other hand, can it be asserted that a diet of rice and bananas constitutes priesthood. In the town called Benares are many bulls who eat nothing else. But these are not priests, inasmuch as they do not cheat. I admit, however, that if cheats eat bananas and rice they are usually regarded as priests.

The essential quality of sacerdotal marriages is that a priest should sit solemnly and be the intermediary between bride and bridegroom. As he sits, he talks rapidly in a sing-song voice. This talk is called 'the marriage ceremony.' I regret to say that I have not been able to procure an actual specimen of the formula used on such occasions, but I gather that the allocution is somewhat as follows:—

"Oh, man and maid, be ye joined in the bonds of matrimony. If ye be thus yoked, I shall never lack sufficiency of rice and bananas. Be ye, then, joined together. On various ritual occasions in the life of this bride I shall then be in a position to intervene, and shall earn more rice and bananas. On even more frequent occasions in the life of your future offspring I shall obtain *much* rice and bananas. Be ye therefore joined together. In your joint existence as heads of a family you will have to perform many and meticulous ceremonies in which you will need my kindly and suitably compensated services. Be ye then indissolubly joined together. Be one flesh; never depart from one another, lest there be any deficiency in my just gains. If ye separate, ye shall meet with condign and degrading punishment. So has the wisdom of our ancestors ordained."

It is, no doubt, from fear of this punishment that sacerdotal marriage is regarded as indissoluble. On the other hand, the form of marriage which is in force among us is called 'irregular' marriage. I cannot say that it is unknown in men's society. There are indeed men and women who make use of *both* forms of marriage. There is, however, this difference, that 'sacerdotal' marriage is never, I think, secretly contracted, whereas the other kind is always very carefully concealed. I understand that if one man happens to become aware that another man has contracted an irregular marriage, he immediately assaults or otherwise persecutes him. There can be little doubt that this is due to priestly instigation, since it is by means of 'sacerdotal' marriage that this variety of men procures rice and bananas. The most remarkable feature of these marriage customs is that men who have themselves entered into irregular unions will unhesitatingly attack those who follow their example. My own personal inference is that the majority of men are secretly in favour of marriage as practised among us, but dare not say so for fear of their 'priests.' I ascertained, during my stay among men, that it is chiefly among the higher orders of men that such unions are in vogue. In other words, ladies and gentlemen, it is the most advanced and refined of mankind who follow the customs of our ancient race in this matter. We may be permitted to hope that social progress among this interesting species may lead to the universal adoption of the more rational and civilised form of union. Indeed many of the wisest and noblest of men, have written books in favour of what has beautifully been called 'Free Love.' May I respectfully suggest that such men of light and leading might be elected honorary members of our Congress? If this could be effected I trust that our younger friends will carefully refrain from regarding our honorary members as articles of food. After all, they resemble us in possessing a genuine, a philosophic instinct for social advancement.

There is one interesting variety of irregular marriage which may be defined as 'pecuniary marriage.' In such cases an interchange of coins occurs between the parties."

Mr. Odontokeros:—"What is coin, pray?"

"Coin is a kind of god worshipped by men. With your kind permission, I should like to say a few words on the subject of this interesting cult. Of all the many deities adored by men, coin is undoubtedly held in the highest reverence. It is represented by very curious images, constructed in gold, silver and copper. For some reason unknown to me, these images are never made of iron, tin, or wood. They are carefully bestowed in receptacles of silk, wool, cotton and leather. Men pay their devotions to them night and day, and are ever occupied in the endeavour to procure access to these miraculous images. Any house in which much coin is known to exist is thronged with eager worshippers. So much so that I have known them to refuse to depart even when assaulted and forcibly ejected. The priest of this deity, if I may so describe those in whose abodes it takes up its habitation, are held in high public regard. If such a dignitary should deign to cast a look on an ordinary man, such a person is filled with modest pride.

It must be admitted that the deity in question is all-powerful and omnipresent in the transactions of men. There is no commodity in use among them that cannot be obtained by its intervention. There is no crime which cannot be committed under its auspices. No fault is there but can be overlooked by invoking its beneficent aid. What virtue is there that is recognised in human society unless it have the indispensable support of coin? He in whose home this most excellent of divinities has taken up its abode may be regarded as infallible. It is the sacred possession of money that constitutes wisdom among men. The scholar, however great his learning, is regarded as a fool if he does not possess the tribal deity. If we speak of a Great Tiger, the term implies the possession of strength, beauty, and valour. But if a man is called Great Man, we are not to suppose that he is eight or ten feet long. No, the expression merely signifies that he has the sacred image in his possession, by whatever means it may be acquired. If a man lacks this advantage, he is called 'a low fellow', no matter what his actual stature may be.

When I first became acquainted with the marvellous qualities of this deity, it occurred to me that I might advocate the extension of its cult to our community. I was deterred, however, by my subsequent investigations. I discovered, alas, that this insidious power is the very root and origin of the calamities of men. Tigers and other leading species of animals do not dislike and envy one another. Far otherwise is it with the miserable race of men. They detest and envy one another to an incredible degree, and the sole cause of this extraordinary state of things is their principal deity. In their greed for its possession, they are always planning the downfall of their fellows. In my previous discourse I told you how thousands of them will meet together to 'wage war', as they call it. It is coin which is the sole cause of this disastrous custom. In the service of this really maleficent deity men inflict death, wounds, disease, slander, envy, malice, and all uncharitableness upon one another. You will not be surprised, then, that on further consideration I gave up all thought of introducing this dangerous and unsocial cult into our happy and innocent community.

But men do not understand this. I have already explained to you that they are naturally addicted to mutual destruction. In the search for the curious round images of gold and silver which they worship, they will shrink from no action, however foolish and unsocial.

There are many other customs of men as irrational and ludicrous as their marriage customs. But I fear to interfere with your 'business' arrangements if I continue my discourse. Perhaps I may have some other opportunity of discussing these matters at greater length."

With these words the learned professor resumed his seat amid a great slapping of tails. An erudite young tiger, Macronyx, [10] by name, rose to open the discussion of the professor's discourse. "Ladies and Gentlemen, it is my pleasing duty to propose a unanimous vote of thanks to the distinguished lecturer. A due regard for scientific accuracy, however, compels me to assert that his lecture was a very poor one and full of ridiculous mistakes. With all due deference, I may be allowed to say that our learned friend is little better than a fool."

Cries of "Order! Order!"

The President: "My young friend will allow me to call his attention to the fact that in polite circles it is not permissible to make use of such uncompromisingly plain speech. In parliamentarly *[sic]* language, of course, even more offensive imputations may properly be made."

Cries of "Hear! Hear!"

Mr. Macronyx: "I bow to the president's ruling. I will gladly say that the lecturer is an eminently truthful person, since though the bulk of his discourse is a tissue of baseless fabrications, one or two of his assertions may be accepted as true. We all admit that he is a distinguished *savant*. Many of us may be of opinion that his discourse contains nothing that was worth saying. But let us be grateful for the instruction we have received from his lips to-day, even if I am reluctantly unable to give my support to all his statements. More particularly, if I may be allowed to say so, he is hopelessly mistaken in the account he has given us of the institution of marriage among men. Among us, if any tiger, with a view to the continuance of the species, consorts with a fair tigress, that constitutes matrimony. (I would beg my learned hearers, in passing, to note the etymology of the word 'consort'. It is made up of *con*, implying union, and *sors*, fate or accident.) The marriage of men is not of this sort. Man is by nature a weak and dependent animal. Hence every man has a need of a superior, and is compelled to appoint a female of his own species to be his guide and ruler. This, gentlemen, is what they call 'matrimony'. When the ceremony is performed in the presence of witnesses, it is called a 'sacerdotal' marriage. The witnesses are known as 'priests'. The rendering of the formulae used on such occasions given by our lecturer is wholly inaccurate.

The true formula may be roughly translated as follows:—

The priest: "Tell me, do you wish me to be witness to this transaction?"

The bridegroom: "Sir, I desire you to be witness to the fact that I take this woman to be my lawful ruler and guide till death do us part."

The priest: "What else?"

The bridegroom: "I hereby promise and vow that I shall be her faithful slave and attendant. I cheerfully assume the task of providing food for our joint sustenance. Her sole duty shall be to eat what I procure."

The priest (to the bride): "What do you say?"

The bride: "I willingly take this man to be my affianced bondslave. So long as he shall be to my liking, I shall permit him to remain in my service. When I no longer desire his aid and companionship, I shall dismiss him without scruple or remorse."

The priest: "Amen, so be it."

But there are many such mistakes in the excellent discourse to which we have attentively listened. For instance, we have been told that coin is an object of worship among men. This is quite inaccurate. Coin is on the contrary a deadly poison. Men are inordinately addicted to the consumption of poisonous and harmfull substances. That is why they collect such great store of coin. Observing their regard for this commodity, I naturally assumed, in my younger days, that it was good to eat. I resolved to make an experiment of its qualities as food. One day, having slain a man on the lovely banks of the Vidyadhari river, I found some coins amongst his clothing. I immediately swallowed them. The next day I suffered severely from indigestion. What doubt, then, can there be that coin is a kind of poison?"

After several other speeches had been delivered, the president closed the proceedings by addressing the following brief but eloquent words to the Congress:—

"Ladies and Gentlemen,

The evening is now far advanced and the usual time for 'business' is at hand. To put the matter in a concrete form, who knows when a herd of deer may present itself? I will not therefore try your patience with a long address. I am sure you will agree with me that the speeches we have heard this evening have been excellent, and we are much obliged to our learned lecturer for supplying us with so interesting and suggestive a subject for discussion. One conclusion we must all have drawn from what we have heard, and that is that men are a very uncivilised species. We, on the other hand, are a highly civilised race. It is our obvious duty to do all that lies in our power to educate and improve the race of men. I humbly believe that it has pleased Providence to send us to this beautiful land of the Sunderbans for no other purpose. Moreover it is not unlikely that the higher men mount in the scale of civilisation, the more tender and delicious will be their flesh, and the more easily we shall be able to capture them. For, the better their education, the more clearly will they understand that the principal object of their existence is to furnish food for tigers. This is the kind of civilisation which it befits us to impart to them. I commit this view of the matter to your attentive consideration. It is the high destiny of the race of tigers, firstly, to educate men, and, secondly, to devour them."

This genial summary of the discussion was received with loud applause, and with a cordial vote of thanks to the president, the meeting dispersed, each departing as his experience or whim led him in search of his own 'business.'

It happened that the place of meeting was surrounded by lofty trees, screened by whose leaves a party of monkeys had silently listened to the discussion. When the tigers had departed, one of these monkeys poked his face through the leaves, and asked,

"Tell me, brother, are you there?"

The other replied, "Sir, at your service!"

The first monkey: "Come along then, and let us talk over what these tiger people have been saying."

The second monkey: "Goodness, why?"

The first monkey: "These tigers are our hereditary enemies. Let us gratify our ancient enmity by saying frankly what we think of them."

The second monkey: "By all means. Frankness of the kind you mean is natural to us monkey folk."

The first monkey: "Very well. But are you sure none of the creatures is still hanging about?"

The second monkey: "No, they are all gone. All the same, we may as well conduct our discussion in the safe shelter of these branches."

The first monkey: "A very proper precaution. Otherwise, if we were recognised, we might some day meet one of these gentlemen, and furnish an untimely meal for his inextinguishable hunger."

The second monkey: "Now what evil have you to say of these brutal tyrants?"

The first monkey: "In the first place, they talk most ungrammatically. We monkeys are admittedly experts in grammar. Their grammar differs lamentably from our monkey grammar."

The second monkey: "True. What else?"

The first monkey: "Their language is very disagreeable to the ear."

The second monkey: "Exactly. They do not use monkey speech."

The first monkey: "For instance, their president used this cumbrous expression, 'it is the high destiny of the race of tigers, firstly, to educate men, and, secondly, to devour them.' Why could he not have said, 'Eat them first and educate them afterwards?' That would have been a much more reasonable remark."

The second monkey: "No doubt, no doubt. Else why are we called monkeys?"

The first monkey: "These people have no idea how to conduct a discussion, or what language to use. During the making of a speech, it is befitting to gibber, to leap from place to place, to screw up the face in an expressive manner, to nibble a banana from time to time. What they ought to do is to take some lessons in oratory from *us*."

The second monkey: "They might then have some hope of being monkeys and not mere tigers."

In the meanwhile some other monkeys took courage to emerge from their hiding-places. One of them remarked:

"In my opinion, the chief fault of the oratory consisted in this that the president, relying on his own unaided wits, made use of various expressions for which there is no precedent in literature. All phrases that have not been carefully chewed and digested by classical authors are extremely faulty. We are monkey folk, and during long ages have spent our time in chewing. That the tiger people have not followed our example must be attributed as sin to them."

At this point a lovely young lady monkey observed, "I could make a list of a thousand faults in the discussion. Hundreds of times I could not understand what they were talking about. What greater fault can there be than to fail to make yourself intelligible to the ladies in the audience?"

Another monkey said, "I am not sure that I can point out any specific errors in all this speechifying. But I can do what no tiger ever did. I can grimace hideously and display my breeding and wit by the use of the foulest and most disgusting abuse."

In such fashion the monkey folk poured scorn on their hereditary foes. A stout elderly monkey closed the discussion by remarking, "What a pity Professor Macrurus cannot hear these scathing criticisms of his lecture! He would no doubt retire to his den, and perish from sheer mortification. Come, my friends; let us go and eat bananas."

---

1. I have substituted Greek names for the Sanskrit polysyllables in the original, which mean Doctor Long-tailed Tiger.—[Translator's note].
2. *Amitodar* or "Boundless-bellied" in the original.
3. *Brihallangul* or "Long-tailed" in the original.
4. *Mahadamstra* or "With-big-teeth" in the original.
5. *Udar-puja* or "Belly-worship" in the original.
6. A Company was formed to establish a new port for Calcutta on the Matla river, which is more easily navigable than the Hooghly. The Company was unsuccessful, and the shareholders lost much money.
7. A common term of abuse.
8. Which in Bengali parlance means that they are behaving like asses, not attending to the real needs of the country.
9. *i.e.* Am I a donkey?
10. *Dirghanakha* or "Long-nails" in the original.

THE GLOBE OF GOLD

[A Humorous Story from the pen of the late Bankim Chandra Chatterjee. Translated by Miriam Singleton Knight]

ON Koylas Peak, beneath the budding Deodars, sat Mahadev and his spouse Parvati, on tiger skins, throwing the dice. The stake was a globe of gold. The fault in Mahadev's play was that he could not win the stake. Had he been able to do so at the churning of the ocean, the poison would not have lodged in his throat.

But Parvati was clever at winning the stake; in proof of which, witness her annual three days' worship on earth. However it might be with the dice, at weeping she was unrivalled, having superhuman capacity in that direction. Thus, if a high throw fell to Mahadev she roused the neighbourhood with her cries, and when a low number fell to herself she would cast at the three-eyed Mahadev a glance calculated to destroy the universe, so that though he got the winning throw, he appeared not to notice it, and lost the stake. This was the invariable result.

So Mahadev consented to bestow upon Parvati the golden ball, which she had no sooner obtained than she threw it down upon the earth: whereupon the five-faced god demanded with a frown, "Why have you thrown away my gift?"

Parvati replied, "Lord! your ball must certainly possess some wonderfully beneficent property. I have cast it down to benefit mankind."

The god made answer, "Lady, no good can result from opposing the laws by which Prajâpati, Vishnu and I have framed the universe. Prosperity can come only from obedience to these laws. A golden ball can serve no purpose. If it have any beneficent property, the laws being broken, it will injure mankind. At your suggestion I have endued it with a special quality. Sit here, and watch how it works."

Kali Kanta Babu was a man of good position, in age about thirty-five, of a goodly presence. Some years earlier he had contracted a second marriage, and he was now on his way to visit his wife, Kama Sundari, a girl about eighteen, now staying at her father's house. His father-in-law was a wealthy man, residing at a village on the banks of the Ganges.

Kali Kanta, fastening his boat to the Ghāt, set out on foot for the house of his father-in-law, attended by his servant, Rama, bearing his portmanteau. Kali Kanta Babu noticed a golden ball lying in the path. Picking it up in astonishment, he found it was indeed of fine gold. Much pleased, he handed it to his servant, saying, "I see this is golden; some one must have lost it. If it is inquired for I will produce it, otherwise, I will take it home with me. For the present, keep it carefully."

In order to conceal the ball in his dress, Rama put down the portmanteau, then taking the golden thing from his master's hand he hid it in his garments. But Rama did not again place the portmanteau on his head. Kali Kanta took it up and placed it on his own head. Rama went on in front, the Babu followed with his load. Presently Rama called out "Hi, you Rama!"

Babu. "What do you wish, Sir?"

Rama. "You are an ill-mannered fellow. Take care that you are guilty of no rudeness in my father-in-law's house. They are gentlefolk."

Babu. "Could I possibly commit any rudeness in your presence?"

In Koylas, Parvati was saying, "My lord! I can't understand this at all. What is this property in your golden ball?"

Mahadev answered, "Its property is exchange of mental personality. If I were to place this ball in Nandi's hand he would think 'I am Mahadev,' and would take me to be Nandi. I should think myself Nandi and fancy Nandi to be Mahadev. Rama thinks, 'I am Kali Kanta Babu,' and takes the Babu to be the servant Rama. Kali Kanta thinks, 'I am Rama Khansama,' and fancies Rama to be Kali Kanta Babu."

When Kali Kanta Babu arrived at the house, his father-in-law was in the inner apartments. But the confusion began outside. The gatekeeper, Ram Din Panre, said, "Hi, Khansamaji, don't sit there, come and sit with us." Whereupon Rama replied angrily, "Go, go you rustic fellow, mind your own business."

The gatekeeper took down the portmanteau from the head of Kali Kanta Babu, who said, "Do not insult the Babu in that manner. He will become angry and go away."

The gatekeeper was acquainted with the son-in-law, but not with the servant, so when he heard Kali Kanta Babu speak thus he thought, "Since the son-in-law speaks of this person as 'Babu,' he must be some great man in disguise." In this faith he addressed Rama humbly, with joined hands, entreating pardon for his fault. To which Rama answered, "Well, well, send some tobacco."

Udbhab Khansama was an ancient servant of the father-in-law's household. He brought a handsomely mounted *huka* prepared for use, which Rama, reclining among the cushions, began to smoke. Kali Kanta, seeking the servants' rooms, enjoyed his modest hubble-bubble. Greatly amazed, Udbhab exclaimed, "What is this, Sir? why do you do thus?" Kali Kanta replied, "How can I smoke in his presence?"

Udbhab going to the inner apartments, said to his master: "The Jamai Babu (son-in-law) has arrived, Sir, and a gentleman in disguise has come with him. The Jamai Babu honours him so highly that he will not even smoke before him."

The head of the house, Nil Ratan Babu, came out in haste. Kali Kanta, seeing him, prostrated himself in the distance and moved away. Rama, coming forward, took a pinch of dust from Nil Ratan Babu's feet, and they mutually embraced. Nil Ratan thought "The companion is certainly a well-bred man, but why does the son-in-law act so strangely?"

Nil Ratan Babu sat down to address the usual welcoming inquiries to his visitor, but could make nothing at all of his replies. Meantime, lunch having been prepared in the inner apartments, a female attendant appeared to call the son-in-law to partake of it. Kali Kanta said, "Good gracious! How can I take food before the Babu has eaten? Let him be served first, then my turn will come; I will eat in your mess, Ma Thakurun."

The maidservant, hearing herself addressed in this respectful manner, thought to herself, "The Jamai Babu takes me for one of the family! Why should he not? I come of respectable people and show it in my looks. He sees all sorts and can distinguish, not like the stupid people in this house, who don't know a gentlewoman when they see one." So, greatly pleased, the maid, Bindi, went inside and reported that the Jamai Babu's scruple was admirable, that it would not be suitable for him to eat until his companion had eaten, that the friend should be served first.

The mistress thought, "This is some stranger, so let him be served outside, and the son-in-law in the inner apartments." Rama, seeing preparations for his lunch in the outer apartments, was much incensed, thinking "What a strange proceeding is this."

In the meantime the maid called Kali Kanta to lunch. All was ready within, but Kali Kanta, standing in the courtyard, said, "Why should I go in? Give me a little pulse and treacle in my hand to eat here."

The sister-in-law said, "What a lot of funny ways you have learned."

Distressed, Kali Kanta replied, "Why do you make fun of me? Am I a fit object for your sport?"

An elder lady said, "Why an object of sport to us? Go to her who has the right to jest with you." And taking his hand, stumbling as she went, she pulled him into the room.

Kali Kanta's wife, Kama Sundari, was standing there. Kali Kanta, taking her to be the wife of his master, prostrated himself before her. At this, Kama Sundari's lovely face broke into smiles. "What game is this?" she asked. "What new jest have you learned?"

Troubled by these words, Kali Kanta said, "Oh! why will you speak to me thus? I am your servant, you are my lord."

"You are servant, I am master? not for to-day or tomorrow only—so long as I live that relation shall continue. Now eat your lunch."

Kali Kanta. "If anyone has represented me to you in that light he has lied. Humbly I beg of you, as my preceptress, to let me go."

Jest-loving Kama Sundari thought this was indeed a new sort of game. She said, "Dearer than life, I begin to see that you have learned some fine jokes this time," and taking his two hands, she again pulled him towards the seat.

No sooner had she caught him by the hand than he, thinking all was over with him, shouted out, "Help! help I am done for! she is killing me!"

The frightened family came running at these cries. Kama Sundari, at the sight of her mother, sister, and aunt, released her husband's hands, and he, seizing this opportunity, with a long breath, escaped.

The mistress asked her daughter, "What is the matter, Kami? Why has the son-in-law gone in this way? Did you strike him?"

Amazed and wounded to the heart, Kama Sundari answered, "I strike him! why should I strike him—with so evil a fate as mine?" Gradually her voice was lost in sobs. "My evil destiny—some wretch has destroyed me—has bewitched him." These cries attracted a crowd around her. They said, "Yes, you must have struck him, else why should he call out so piteously?" And they called her names—"sinful one," "witch," "ogress," &c., scolding her. The innocent Kama Sundari, thus reproached, went weeping to her room, closed the door, and laid herself down on her bed.

Meantime, Kali Kanta, coming out, saw that a great commotion had arisen. Nil Ratan Babu himself, the gate keeper, and Udbhab, were all belabouring Rama wherever they chanced to find him. Amid the shower of slaps and cuffs raining upon him, Rama kept saying, "Let me go, I never heard of a son-in-law being beaten so; it does not matter to me, but do you want to make your daughter a widow?"

Near by stood Taranga, the maid servant, laughing. She was accustomed to go to the son-in-law's house, and told her master that she recognised the man as being the Babu's servant, Rama. Kali Kanta Babu, seeing the beating going on, paced the courtyard like one distraught, crying, "How dreadful! they are beating the Babu!"

At this, Nil Ratan Babu, yet more enraged, said to Rama, "You, fellow! what have you given the son-in-law to eat to madden him? Beat the rascal with a shoe!"

At this command, as rain follows rain in August, so on the guiltless Rama fell the rain of blows. In the pain of the beating, the ball hidden in his garments fell to the ground. The maid, Taranga, picking it up, offered it to her master, saying, "This good-for-nothing fellow is a thief! See, Sir, he has stolen a golden ball." "Let me see it," said Nil Ratan Babu, taking it from her. Then, letting Rama go, he stood aside, opened the pleated fold of his upper garment, and cast it over his head (like a woman's veil), while Taranga, letting her *sari* fall from her head, tucked it up like a man's, and was about to beat Rama with the slipper, when Udbhab said to her, "You, woman, why are you again mixing yourself up with this?"

Taranga. "Whom are you calling woman?"

Udbhab. "You!"

Taranga. "You mock at me!" and, with the slipper in her hand, she struck Udbhab. He, greatly incensed, but unwilling to strike a woman, looked towards his master, saying, "See, Sir, the impudence of this woman, she is striking me with a shoe!"

But the master, pulling his veil a little more over his face, with a merry smile, said, sweetly, "Yes, he is striking you; but do not be angry. He is the master, and may do so."

Whereat Udbhab, yet more incensed, replied, "How is she my master? She is a servant, I also am a servant. How can you talk like this? I am your servant; how can I be hers? I don't serve on those terms."

Again, smiling merrily, the master said, in the same gentle voice, "What curious fancies we see in old men! My servant! how can you be that?"

Speechless with amazement, Udbhab thought, "Have we got into a lunatic neighbourhood to-day?" And in his surprise he let go Rama, and remained standing.

At this moment, Gobordhan Ghosh, keeper of the household cows, came up—he was Taranga's husband. He was astonished at Taranga's condition and behaviour, also she took no notice of him: while, on the other hand, the master of the house, seeing Gobordhan, again drew the veil off his face and stood aside. Looking sideways at Gobordhan, he whispered, "Don't mix yourself up in that."

Gobordhan, witnessing Taranga's conduct, became enraged; the master's words did not reach his ear. He went to seize Taranga by the hair, "Vile woman!" he exclaimed; "have you no shame?" Seeing him coming, Taranga said, "Gobordhan! are you also out of your senses? go and feed the cows!"

At this Gobordhan seized her by the hair, and began to abuse her roundly, whereupon Nil Ratan Babu exclaimed, "Heavens! that ill-fated wretch is murdering the master."

Taranga, also becoming furious, said, "Do you dare to touch the person of your master?" and began to strike Gobordhan.

Then the uproar became general. At the sound of it the neighbours, Ram Mukherji, Gobind Chatterji, &c., came up to see what was going on. Ram Mukherji, seeing a golden ball lying about, took it up and gave it to Gobind Chatterji, saying, "See, Sir, what is this?"

In Koylas, Parvati now said, "Oh, my lord! take back your golden ball, only see! Gobind Chatterji has gone into old Ram Mukherji's inner apartments, and taking the old man's old wife to be his own young wife is addressing sportful speeches to her; and Ram Mukherji's scandalised maid servants are beating the intruder with a broom. Meanwhile, old Ram Mukherji, fancying himself the youthful Gobind Chatterji, has gone to Gobind's inner rooms, and is singing songs to Gobind's wife. Should that ball remain a moment longer in the world there will be confusion in every house. Therefore take it back."

Mahadev answered, "Oh, mountain born! what is the fault in my ball? Is this a new condition of things on earth? Do you not constantly observe the old setting the young in order, the young doing the same by the old? The master behaving like the servant, the servant in his master's seat? Do you never see a man behaving like a woman, or a woman like a man? All these things are constantly happening on the earth, but no one seems to see how ludicrous it is. I have for once made it evident to the senses of all. Now, I take back the ball. At my wish each shall return to his own nature, and no one shall remember what has occurred."